W9-DJH-508

The River Whispers

Pamela Pizzimenti

AuthorHouse™
1663 Liberty Drive, Suite 200
Bloomington, IN 47403
www.authorhouse.com
Phone: 1-800-839-8640

First published by AuthorHouse 8/22/2008

ISBN: 978-1-4343-7570-4 (sc)

Library of Congress Control Number: 2008906287

Printed in the United States of America
Bloomington, Indiana

This book is printed on acid-free paper.

I wish to express my appreciation to my husband, Craig, for encouraging me to take on this venture. Thank you Dru, Arthur, Sage, and Cora; you inspire me on a daily basis. I dedicate this book to those people who touch our lives and then move on, but leave us with memories, life lessons, and love.

Chapter 1
First-Day Jitters

The first thing that struck me as odd that first day at Turnville School was crossing the campus in the morning among much younger children. I had gotten used to being on a junior high school campus, so to have first and second graders passing me in the hallway felt weird. Plus it made me feel so much younger. Any independence that I thought I'd found was snatched away from me. I wouldn't be shuffling between six classes anymore either; there were only two eighth-grade classes at Turnville School.

I found my classroom and glanced around the room as I entered. A few kids were seated and chatting with each other. I walked up the second aisle toward an empty desk. My eyes gravitated to a boy in the fourth seat. He looked younger than the other kids in the class—shorter, with a small frame, a thin face, and pasty white skin. It crossed my mind that perhaps he was ill or something.

As I passed the boy, I looked directly into his eyes. They were a soft, warm green. His disheveled hair was a deep brown. He returned my stare with a look of disbelief. As I plopped myself into the seat behind him, I felt embarrassed for having stared so impolitely. He swiveled completely around in his seat, throwing his arm over the back of his chair in an easy manner. With a relaxed smile he said, "Hi."

I replied with a "Hi there."

The relaxed expression on his face twisted into a look of joyous surprise. It was like watching a toddler chase after a floating balloon ... that look of delight. His reaction seemed a bit over the top to me.

A girl two seats ahead of me turned around and said hi to me too. Perhaps this year wouldn't be as bad as I had anticipated. I mean, everyone seemed friendly enough.

A tall, blond-haired boy entered the room. He appeared awkward and clumsy as he lumbered down the aisle.

"Hey, Johnny," a boy yelled from across the room. "Glad to see we got you instead of that brother of yours in our class this year." A few laughs burst out from around the room, and Johnny dismissed the comment with a sheepish grin. I had no idea what they were talking about, and that feeling of being out of place flushed over me again.

Johnny stopped in front of me and made eye contact with me. I looked down at the desk and felt my cheeks burn. I glanced back up just as he plopped himself down in the seat in front of me. He sat right on top of ... no, not on top of, it was more like he sat right through the small, frail-looking boy. It was as if the boy in front of me had just disappeared like smoke disperses in the wind.

I heard a scream, not even realizing it was me. It was like one of those out-of-body experiences you hear about. A spinning, warping sort of sensation came over me, and I felt nauseated, like something was squeezing in the pit of my stomach. The room seemed to be tilting, so I moved with it and fell completely out of my seat. Then everything went black.

Sounds were the first thing to make sense, voices mumbled around me. I was afraid to open my eyes. The words became clearer and I deciphered what people were saying around me—about me. I couldn't identify who was speaking because I still didn't know anyone.

"Someone get a wet paper towel," I heard a woman say, "and Johnny, run to the office and get Nurse Jillian. Be quick."

"Move out of the way. She can't breathe with everyone hovering over her." That voice sounded like the voice of the boy who had disappeared.

"What's her problem anyhow?" a girl in the room remarked.

"What a freak!" someone said, followed by a few agreeing sounds.

With a sense of dread I opened my eyes and tried to focus.

"Are you okay?" Leaning over me was a pleasant-looking woman with short brown hair. She had the kind of short haircut that was just over her ears, which my friends and I always referred to as the "mom 'do." I missed my friends from Oceanside terribly at that moment, because *they* wouldn't be calling me a freak, *they* would have been concerned about me.

"I'm Ms. Roberts, your teacher. Can you stand up? Let me help you." I moved to get up, but I still felt woozy and sat back down on the floor. I leaned against a desk. My head ached — my heart ached. Why did I have to move to this stupid place anyway?

Ms. Roberts said, "I think you hit your head on one of the desks. It's bleeding. Let's get you to the nurse's office."

Johnny, the one who had started this whole thing by sitting through that other boy, entered the room and said, "The nurse is on her way."

"Thank you, Johnny," Ms. Roberts said to the boy. "Here, you're strong—why don't you give me hand." With Johnny on one side of me and Ms. Roberts on the other, I felt myself being pulled up like a rag doll from the floor. Then together, they guided me out of the classroom and down the hallway. I felt some relief just being out of the room. I became aware of Johnny's arm around me, and the burning sensation in my cheeks came back.

We met up with the nurse halfway down the hall. The nurse took over on my left side where Johnny had been, and the two women continued to help me toward the nurse's office. Johnny went the other way back to class. I looked over my shoulder and saw him glance back at me at the same moment. I was embarrassed to be caught looking at him, but I could have sworn he actually seemed concerned about me.

In the nurse's office Ms. Roberts said to the nurse, "I can't leave my class unattended for long."

"It's under control," replied Nurse Jillian. "She'll stay here. I'll call home. Go ahead, return to class."

Ms. Roberts looked over at me. "Well, Evelyn ... I hope you feel better, and I look forward to having you in my class this year." It seemed like an odd thing to say, but then, what else could she say to a new student who had just passed out in her class?

Just as she reached the door, I said, "Evie. Please call me Evie."

"Okay, Evie." She smiled and walked out of the nurse's office.

Nurse Jillian had me sit on a cot as she cleaned the cut on my forehead and placed a large bandage on it. "Looks like you're getting quite a bump where you hit your head. Can you tell me what happened?"

I had no idea how to explain what I'd seen. I told her that I really didn't know what had happened, that I'd felt dizzy and everything had just gone black. It was mostly the truth.

"A student said you screamed," she said.

"I guess I just felt frightened when everything went black." It was the only response I could think of.

"Hmm ... Did you eat breakfast this morning?" she asked.

"Yes," I answered.

"Well, I'm going to call your mother. Maybe it's best you go home today and get some rest." She stepped out of the room into an attached office, where I could see her sit down and pick up the phone. I heard her speak to someone on the phone. "Yes, this is Nurse Jillian. Could you look up the phone number of a new student?" I assumed she was talking to someone in the front office. I fell back onto the cot, closed my eyes, and imagined just how furious my mother was going to be. Not only was this my first day of school, but it was her first day at her new job as bank manager.

I opened my eyes and saw the small, pale boy I had seen earlier sitting on top of a file cabinet. I quickly sat up and hunched against the wall.

"You *can* see me. This is great!" he said excitedly. "I knew it when you sat behind me in the classroom." He hopped off the cabinet and started pacing. "I haven't had anyone to talk to for two years. ... This is great!" He turned and looked at me. "What's your name? Where are you from? Where do you live? This is great!"

All he could say was how great this was. I sat frozen with my eyes wide like saucers, too stunned to move. I finally croaked out a hoarse whisper. "Who are you? What's going on?"

Nurse Jillian hung up the phone, stood up, and walked toward me. She stopped in the doorway between the two rooms. The boy was standing between us. She said, "What's that, dear? I didn't hear what you asked. I was on the phone."

I cleared my throat, but my voice still came out shaky. "Uh, I was just wondering, how many people are in this room right now?"

She looked at me suspiciously before she answered in a slow, drawn-out manner, "Just you and I are here." When I didn't say anything, she nodded and continued, "Perhaps the sooner you get home and get some rest the better." She turned around and returned to the phone to call my mother.

I stared in disbelief at the boy.

"My name's David," he said, "and the fact that you can see me is the greatest thing that has happened to me in a long time." I stayed silent. I refused to answer David again in front of the nurse.

Nurse Jillian escorted me to the parking lot, where my mother was waiting. My mother didn't say much; she mostly nodded while Nurse Jillian spoke. Once the nurse was finished filling my mother in on the events of the morning, my mother turned to her and thanked her. I kept my head down and climbed into the front passenger seat of the car. Out the side window I watched Nurse Jillian return to her office. My mother walked around the back of the car, opened the door, and sat behind the steering wheel.

With a loud sigh my mother put the key in the ignition. I looked down at my feet and remained quiet. When my mother had spoken with the nurse, she had been polite and courteous, but I knew my mother well, and I knew she was ticked off. There was nothing I could say to change her being angry with me. The most bizarre part was that David sat in the backseat observing everything.

David had finally gotten the message that I wasn't going to answer him, but he wouldn't go away. Back at the nurse's office he had continued to talk to me and I had continued to ignore him. Now as he sat in the backseat he appeared as patient as a spider waiting for a fly to land in its web.

As we drove out of the school parking lot, the silence in the car was so thick you could have sliced it with a knife. The heavy silence reminded me of the uncomfortable car trip that my mother and I had taken just four weeks earlier. It had been a stifling hot day when my mother and I had driven to the cemetery to bury Nonno, my grandpa. That car ride had had the same kind of tangible silence.

From the passenger window I critically sized up the town of Turnville. It seemed dumpy. A faded river resort town that no tourists seemed to care about anymore. The buildings were all dull colors like brown, dark green, and gray. The first time we had driven through town, my mother had said how quaint it was, but to me it just seemed worn out. My eyes shifted from the buildings downtown to the side mirror. My hair was a mess now. I had spent all morning trying to look nice, wanting desperately to make a good impression at my new school, and now I looked a wreck! I wanted to cry, but I was too worn out to cry anymore, worn out like the town.

Although no tears flowed, I felt the welling around the base of my eyes. I remembered what my Nonno had always said about my eyes. He called them "mood eyes." My eyes are hazel, but sometimes they look green and other times they appear blue. He said that when I was excited about something, the blue would shine through, and that when I was sad and had been crying, my eyes seemed greener. I stared at my reflection and noticed that my eyes were definitely greener.

I swallowed back my desire to cry and glanced at the backseat to see if David was still there. He was. I kept turning around to look at him, hoping each time that he would be gone, but he would shrug and smile. My mother's eyes darted to the rearview mirror trying to see what I was looking at. Finally, she broke the silence.

"I can't believe these dramatics, Evie.... What is wrong with you? You know this is my first day as bank manager." She sucked in a long, deep breath and I could tell she was trying to stay calm. My mother didn't like emotional outbursts. She continued in her calm, deliberate voice, "I know that you're not happy with this move, but you're not even trying ..."

"Mom," I interrupted, "you wouldn't believe me if I did tell you what really happened."

"Try me. Help me understand. Convince me that there *is* a good reason for pulling me away from my first day at work." Her rational way of speaking made me feel like a small child and filled me with guilt.

I told her the truth. I told her about seeing David and how the other boy had sat through him and how David had disappeared. I told her about how I saw David in the nurse's office and how the nurse didn't see him. I was just about to tell her that David was sitting in the car when she cut me off. She completely gave up on her calm voice and belted out, "Evie, stop this nonsense right now!"

She pulled the car to the side of the road, right in front of the entrance to our street, Cherry Lane. She took another deep breath. "There's going to be a lot of adjustments … for both of us, but making up stories to get attention isn't going to solve anything"—her mouth turned down at the edges—"and it certainly isn't going to bring Nonno back." My heart did ache terribly from missing Nonno, but couldn't she tell that this wasn't about Nonno? Couldn't she see that I was telling the truth? That David was real? I gave up. She wasn't going to believe me, and I didn't know how to convince her otherwise.

"I need to get back to work. Are you feeling well enough to walk down the street to the house?" she asked.

"Sure." I snatched my backpack, and moved to get out of the car.

She grabbed my wrist when I was halfway out of the car and forced me to look her in the eyes. "Evie, I love you," she said. "Call me at the bank when you get home, okay?" I nodded.

I stood at the side of the road as she turned the car around, then watched her drive away, back toward town. With David unfortunately still at my side, we turned around and started walking down Cherry Lane together.

Chapter 2
Myths and Mystery

Cherry Lane was a one-lane road just outside town that wound between redwoods along a seasonal creek. Our new house was about two miles down the road.

"I don't know why you can see me, Evie," David said, "but it's exciting and there must be a reason. I'm sure if you and I put our heads together, we can figure this out, but you have to stop ignoring me."

I stopped in my tracks and turned to face him. I sized him up again, and found that my first impression of him remained true. He was unusually pale and quite short—more than half a foot shorter than me. However, this time I noticed a look of desperation in his warm eyes, a pleading look. "Fine!" I burst out. "But first fill me in. Who are you or *what* are you, a ghost or something?"

"That's exactly what I am," David said, and he proceeded to tell me about how he had died two years earlier on the first day of school.

It had happened the same year Turnville experienced one of the worst river floods ever. Many town residents had spent the summer trying to restore businesses and buildings, tourism was down, and the town was struggling. When school started in the fall, the streets were unusually packed with traffic because of all the construction projects. Most parents preferred to drive their kids to school the first day, but David was walking.

David told me he couldn't remember much. He had heard a screeching sound, seen a flash of white, then felt a strong, heavy sensation. Something slammed into him. He described the feeling of flying through the air in slow motion but never landing, as if he'd just kept floating away.

"You were hit by a car?" I asked.

"Yeah, I think that's what happened."

"What do you mean you *think* so? Don't you *know?*"

David paused before speaking. "No, not really. It's as if my memory's been erased, as if someone hypnotized me and I can't remember. All I really know is that one day I was part of everything and the next day no one could see me anymore." David lowered his head and tried to kick a rock on the road, but missed.

"So why do you think you're still here?" I asked. "Two years seems like a long time."

"You're telling me!" David exclaimed. "It's strange actually. There are gaps in what's happened over the last two years, like I'm not always here, but I can't remember any other place I've been. And when I am here, I can't seem to leave town. What I do know is that I've been going to school. I sat through sixth and seventh grades with no one seeing me. That is, until today."

I rolled my eyes at the thought of it. I had met a ghost who might possibly be able to do and maybe even go just about anywhere he wanted, and he chose to go to school?

That's just crazy! I then understood why he looked so much smaller than me. He probably looked the same as the day he'd died two years prior.

As if reading my thoughts David said, "I'm stuck." I could hear the frustration in his voice. "For some reason I can't leave Turnville."

We walked in silence for a while, both of us lost in thought and unsure what to say next. Then an idea struck me.

I stopped walking and looked at David. "Maybe I can see you so I can help you leave this place and ... I don't know ... 'move on,' as they say. You know, find out what's keeping you here and then you can go to wherever you're supposed to go when you die—heaven, your next adventure, your nirvana, or whatever is supposed to be next."

"And just how do you plan to do that?" he asked.

"I don't know. I don't exactly have a lot of experience with ghosts ... outside of those written about by Shakespeare or found in mythology," I replied.

David perked up. "You like mythology?" he asked. "My favorite is the story about Icarus and his father, Daedalus."

As we walked down the street where no one could see us, I started to feel comfortable talking with David. He was charming, funny, and smart. David seemed to love mythology as much as I did. We compared what we knew about Perseus and Medusa, of Hades and Persephone, and many other Greek myths. We found subtle differences between our versions of the stories. We shifted gears to Egyptian mythology, and that's when I figured out a way to help him.

We were talking about how Isis had discovered that Set had killed Osiris. Isis traveled throughout Egypt collecting pieces of her dead husband. Perhaps I needed to collect pieces of information about David's death and discover who had killed him, much like Isis had done. It was clear that David didn't know what had really happened the day he died and who had killed him.

"That's a great idea!" David exclaimed after I explained my idea. "But how are we going to do that?"

"I don't know yet. I'm going to need a little time to figure out a plan."

David had a great sense of humor, and we made light of his death and the mystery that surrounded it. We compared the driver of the car that hit him to Osiris's brother Set. Under most circumstances it would have been tasteless to joke around about death, but since I was with a ghost, it didn't seem so morbid. Still, there was a part of me that realized that there was someone out there responsible for David's death. Was that person still living in Turnville? Was it someone David knew? Maybe I'd even met this person already. There was a real mystery to solve.

While thinking about David's death we passed a creepy-looking driveway. It was paved with gravel, and the edges were unkempt and overgrown with berry bushes and large wild ferns. At the driveway's entrance a sign dangled from a redwood tree that read HANDMADE FURNITURE OR SPECIALTY WOODWORK. I had been in town only a few days, and I had already heard about the guy who lived there. Big Art Carter, they called him.

The grocery clerk had chatted away with my mom and me when we'd first arrived in Turnville. She'd asked if we were visitors or new to town. She'd come across as nosy. She'd wanted to know where my mother would be working, where we moved from, where our house was, and on and on. Once she'd found out we would be living on Cherry Lane, she'd told us about the town recluse, Art Carter. She warned us that he was as mean as a cornered mountain lion and that we had best stay clear of him, but then she had added in a forced, cheery tone, "Unless, of course, you need some furniture or woodwork done … He does do fine work." I found myself staring at the sign hanging in the tree and thinking there could be no woodwork fine enough to get me to walk down that driveway and hire Art Carter.

The spookiness of the place sent a chill down my spine. Since David and I had been joking around, I made a wisecrack as we passed the house. I pointed to the sign and said, "I wonder if he's like Geppetto, and he's busy trying to carve a real boy out of wood."

David stopped and stared at me. One moment we were kidding around and the next moment his whole demeanor changed. He shoved his hands in his pockets, looked down at his feet, and continued walking sullenly. He groaned, "Maybe he is, Evie. … Maybe he is."

I trotted to catch up with him. I could tell my comment had upset him. "I didn't mean anything by it," I said.

"I know," he said faintly, "but he's *my* father."

David explained that his father had been different before David died. His father used to build houses and had his own business as a contractor. He was often hired to jack houses up, raising them so that they would be above the floodplain. David told me how he had gone to see his father a few times after he died, but that his father couldn't see him. He spoke of the heartache he felt when he saw his father depressed, bitter, and angry. I sensed that David felt responsible for his father's anger and was frustrated that he couldn't do anything about it.

"Do you know why I like the myth of Icarus so much?" he asked rhetorically. "It's because it's very much like my father and me. The day I died he had to leave early to get to a job site. That's why I walked to school that day—he usually dropped me off. My father warned me to be careful and to cross in the crosswalk. Just like Daedalus warned Icarus not to fly too close to the sun." David paused, then said more to himself than to me, "I wish I'd listened, just as my father probably wishes that he had driven me to school.

"My father could create spectacular things with wood. He made the most incredible tree house, and I had a bunk bed that surpassed any child's dream, like a fort and a castle all in one. He tried to teach me how to work wonders out of wood, perhaps in the same fashion that Daedalus tried to teach Icarus. But I was never very good at it ... except one time.

"When I was about seven years old, together my dad and I made this beautiful wooden boat. We had cut, sanded, glued, and painted for months. When it was finished, we walked down to the river and he told me to place it in the water. At first it was exciting to watch what we had created float upon the water and see the river carry it, but when I realized that the current was carrying the boat out of reach, I waded into the water to retrieve it. My father grabbed my arm and held me back. He told me to let it go. He said that the beauty wasn't in keeping it, but in letting it fulfill the purpose for which we had built it. I was heartbroken. It was the only beautiful thing I had ever made, and he forced me to let go of it."

I listened to David talk about letting go, and yet it seemed it was the one thing none of us were doing. I didn't want to let go of Nonno or my old life. David couldn't let go of living. And Art Carter couldn't let go of David. All of it filled me up with sadness.

We arrived at the little house where my mother and I lived and walked up the few steps onto the front deck. It was a fairly large deck under the redwoods, with enough room for an outside set of table and chairs and two chaise lounges. I felt awkward having David there, but it was obvious he felt completely at ease. I stopped at the front door. "Okay," I said, "we need to make some ground rules."

"Like what?" he asked.

"Like ... my house is off limits for you," I said.

"Why?"

"I need a place to think, a place where you won't just pop up and start talking to me, a place where I have some sense of things being normal," I answered. "Besides, it's where I get dressed, shower ... eat ..."

"Okay, okay," David interrupted. "I understand—you need some privacy—but if you're going to set some rules, then I should be allowed to set some too." I was reluctant to answer, but eventually I agreed.

He said, "You'll help me contact my father."

"WHAT?"

Chapter 3
Ignorance Isn't Bliss

I woke up the next morning feeling extremely tired. I'd had a restless night with little sleep because the unusual events of the previous day had raced through my mind all night.

As my mother drove me to school, I thought perhaps I hadn't really met David. I hoped the entire thing had just been some delusion caused from bumping my head. However, when I walked into the classroom, there was David sitting in the back of the room. He waved to me, and I held back the urge to return a wave.

I found a desk in the back of the room in the opposite corner from David, hoping to avoid him. It didn't do any good, because David walked over and sat in the desk next to me.

"Today, right, Evie?" he asked. "Today after school you'll go visit my dad?"

"All right," I mumbled softly. A few students turned to look at me. I grimaced a fake smile and tried to appear as normal as possible. I pulled out a piece of paper and wrote a note to David asking him to stop talking to me in class. I was tired of everyone thinking I was some freak. He read it over my shoulder, then nodded.

At the front of the classroom Ms. Roberts busily gathered things together and prepared for the day's lessons. At the sound of the bell, the talking in class subsided and the school day began.

Throughout the morning I kept my head down and my mouth shut and tried to melt into the background. I wanted to bring as little attention to myself as possible, which wasn't easy, considering the events from the previous day. From time to time someone in the class would turn and glance at me. It was all too obvious that most of these kids had grown up together and I was the outsider. I could only imagine what they were saying.

At lunchtime I avoided everyone and everyone seemed content to avoid me, except for David. I carried my lunch tray to an empty table in the cafeteria, sat down, and picked at my food while David went on about his plan for me to talk to his father after school. Finally I slammed my milk down and yelled at him, "Why can't you just leave me alone?" An uncomfortable silence fell over the cafeteria. I could feel all the stares piercing through me like the concentrated sun stream burning through a magnifying glass. I stood, picked up my tray, and threw it in the garbage as I stormed out of the cafeteria.

I marched across campus to an empty bench. I wanted to cry. David sat next to me. I turned to him, not caring for the moment how crazy I looked. "Look, David, I want to help you, but you need to make this a little easier somehow." Before David could answer, a girl sat down on him. ... No, again it was right through him. This time it just didn't seem as strange. ... Was I getting used to this?

A wide grin stretched across the girl's face as she spoke. "Maybe you'd like someone to sit here so it looks like you're actually talking to someone else?"

I was struck dumb for a moment. "Uh ... thanks," I said.

She looked at me with huge brown eyes. There was a sparkle to them that made her appear as if she were hiding some incredible secret, yet her overall appearance was ordinary, almost mousy. Her long red hair was in a French braid down to the middle of her back. She wore a tie-dye T-shirt and faded denim overalls. One of her tennis shoes had a hole over the big toe, and I could see a bright pink sock poking through. She reminded me of a cross between Pippi Longstocking and a hippie from the '60s.

She extended her hand and confidently introduced herself. "My name's Bliss."

I shook her hand. "Evie," I replied.

"Yes, I know. ... It seems everyone already knows about you." This did not strike me as being a good thing. "Who were you just talking to?" she asked.

It was strange, but I felt like I could tell her the truth. Maybe it was her big, brown, deer-like eyes that made her appear so trustworthy. I looked at David for some guidance, but he just shrugged. So I told her the truth; I told her about David. When I was finished, she remained silent for a long moment as if taking in all the new information. Then she said, "I believe you."

"You do?" I stuttered. "C-c-can ... can you see him too?" I asked.

"Oh no, but I believe you can," Bliss said. "I mean, there are lots of things in life people can't see but they still believe exist. Ghosts, fairies, even God." She took a bite of an apple and sat back with her feet crossed. "You know, I remember David Carter. I'm assuming that he's the David you're seeing." She was talking and chewing on the piece of apple at the same time. "I didn't hang out with him or anything, but he was always nice to me ... and he was smart too." She shook the apple core at me to put an emphasis on her statement.

David pointed to Bliss. "I like her," he said. "She seems to know a good thing when she sees it."

I ignored him and asked Bliss, "Do you remember the day he died?"

"I didn't see it happen. By the time I got to school, the police cars and ambulance had already roped off the area. Other kids talked about seeing a white car take off after the accident." I watched Bliss as she talked. She seemed so comfortable with herself, I envied her. She would have been pretty if she had let her hair down and styled it, and if her clothes were more fashionable, but she didn't seem to care.

A surge of excitement jolted through me when she mentioned the white car. "Did they have any suspects?" I asked.

"Not that I remember, but they did add the second crosswalk in front of the school afterward," she said.

I wondered if I should tell her why I thought I could see David, and then I just blurted out, "Well, I think I'm supposed to help David figure out who killed him, so he can move on."

"Oooh"—she smiled with a dimple on her left cheek—"a mystery. I love a good mystery!" She sat back up with a new interest. "Can I help you? Who knows, it could be fun."

I nodded enthusiastically. I was feeling better already. It was nice to have someone believe me.

The bell rang, signaling the end of lunchtime. Bliss said, "You're in Ms. Roberts's class, right?" I nodded, and she continued with that twinkle in her eyes, "Well, I'm in the other eighth-grade class. Why don't you meet me here after school and we'll devise a plan to solve this mystery."

Bliss and I met after school and discovered that we didn't live very far from each other. She lived on the opposite side of the creek, but closer to the main road. We walked home together and discussed sleuthing on the way.

Bliss had a bounce to her step that made her comical to watch. As we walked, she pushed up on her toes every time she spoke. She was asking David questions, wanting to know what he remembered from the accident. The conversation was awkward at first; Bliss would bounce and ask the question, David would answer it, and then I would have to relay the answer to Bliss. I felt like an echo. The three of us must have been quite a sight: bounce, ask, answer, echo ... bounce, ask, answer, echo ... over and over again.

As comical as it seemed, it was clear to me that Bliss really did believe that David existed. Here she was asking questions of a ghost that she couldn't even see or hear.

"Think hard, David," Bliss said as she bounced. "You remember the car being white, but were there any marks on the car? Do you remember the color of the interior? Was the bumper white or chrome? How old was the car? How many people were in the car? Can you think of anything else that might help?"

I looked at David. He stopped walking, so I stopped walking, then Bliss stopped (mid-bounce), and the three of us stood there. David closed his eyes, put his hand to his forehead, and then said, "I think that there was a woman driving, but I'm not really sure." He shook his head in frustration.

Bliss waited patiently, and then I echoed like a parrot, "He said he thinks a woman was driving, but he's not sure."

"That's great!" Bliss exclaimed, and she took another step with more bounce than before. "That gives us a little more to work with."

"What else can we do?" I asked.

We formulated a plan. First, we would go to the police station and try to get a copy of the police report; maybe there would be information in the report that could help us, like a list of witnesses or something. Second, we would be on the watch for white cars in town, and write down makes, models, years, owners, and anything else we noticed.

When we reached the bridge that crossed the creek, Bliss turned down the street immediately before the bridge. I started to cross the bridge to Cherry Lane on the other side. Bliss turned around, walked backward, and yelled out to me, "Hey, Evie, do you want to come over to my place for a while?" She pointed over her shoulder, then waved for me to catch up with her.

David looked at me with exasperation and demanded, "Evie, you promised you would talk to my dad today!"

"I will," I said to David, "... just later." Then I ran and caught up with Bliss.

We had walked only about quarter mile when Bliss stopped. It was unexpected; she stopped right in front of a small trailer park. I tried not to look too surprised or disappointed.

About a month before, I had envisioned the start of the school year as being exciting. I had pictured starting school with my old friends in Oceanside, being vice president of the school surf club, putting on makeup, getting ready for dances, going to the pier with Nonno after school. Instead here I was stuck in the middle of nowhere and my only friends were a ghost and Hippie Longstocking, who lived in a trailer park.

I knew my thoughts were unfair, that they were cruel and judgmental. Bliss was the only person who believed me—heck, she was the only person who even talked to me. Who was I to judge her for where she lived? I felt ashamed.

Bliss grabbed my hand. "C'mon, I see my mom in the garden." She dragged me to the back of the trailer park to a large vegetable garden. I recognized some of the plants—tomatoes, peppers, and zucchini—but there were others that were unfamiliar to me. As we approached her mom, Bliss pointed at plants and I learned what eggplant, cucumbers, and basil looked like.

Bliss's mom was crouched down, pulling weeds. She wore a sundress with a patchwork of colors and large front pockets. Her long blond hair was pulled back in a French braid, in the same style as Bliss's, and she had on a large straw hat. Her mom waved at us with that already familiar broad smile. Her big brown eyes sized me up with that same sparkling quality as Bliss's. The sun poked through the holes of her hat, creating small shadows that mixed in with a spattering of freckles across her face. Bliss looked like a smaller version of her mother except for the hair color.

"Who's your friend, Bliss?" her mother asked, pushing on her knee to help her stand up.

"This is Evie. She's new at school, she's in Ms. Roberts's class, she lives on Cherry Lane, and she sees a ghost."

My mouth dropped open in shock. Why would Bliss tell her mother that? I was so embarrassed. I clenched my hands, looked down at my feet, and waited to hear how crazy I was, or that maybe Bliss shouldn't be hanging out with me.

Bliss's mom looked at me and nodded. "Really?" she said. "A ghost? That's a special gift." She walked over to me, wiped her hands on the side of her dress, and then extended her hand. "It's nice to meet you, Evie. Call me Maggie." I shook Maggie's hand. She had a firm grip, and I saw that broad smile return to her face. Maggie went back to pulling weeds from around the pepper plants. The reaction was nothing like my mother's. I didn't know if Maggie really believed I could see a ghost or if she was just being nice, but either way I felt relieved that she hadn't made a big deal out of it.

At the back of the garden was a makeshift bench made out of an old board and some upside-down buckets. The bench overlooked the creek, and I saw David sitting on the bench facing me with his arms crossed and a scowl on his face. He was mad that I wasn't going to his father's house, and I knew I was avoiding the task. What was I going to say to his dad? "Excuse me, sir, you don't know me, but I have a message from your dead son"? That just didn't seem reasonable or like a very good idea. I was scared down to the tips of my toes to face Art Carter.

Maggie hollered over to us, "There are fresh cucumbers in the fridge if you girls are hungry." Bliss entered the trailer closest to us and came out with a Tupperware container.

Bliss and I sat on the folding chairs in front of the trailer. Between us, sitting on its side, was a large wooden spool that was once used to hold industrial wire. She placed the container on the spool-table and lifted the lid off. Inside were peeled and sliced cucumbers in a clear liquid. At first I thought the cucumbers were soaking in water to keep them fresh. My mother prepared sliced carrots that way. But when I took a bite into the cucumber, the taste was sour. I crunched more and the taste became sweet. It was delicious! The fresh taste of the cucumber mixed in with the sour taste was unusual, but divine.

"What's that sour taste?" I asked.

"Oh, that's my mom's special way of fixing cucumbers. It's basil and white vinegar with a tad of garlic." It was the vinegar. They were the best cucumbers ever. We gobbled the entire contents of the container in a matter of minutes.

While I was chewing on my last cucumber, the door of the trailer swung open with a slam. I almost choked and jumped clear out of my seat. In the doorway stood a redheaded toddler about two years old. He held a sippy cup in one hand and rubbed his eyes with the other.

"Buzzy!" Bliss exclaimed as she ran over and scooped the little boy into her arms. I was still coughing, as the vinegar burned my throat.

"This is my little brother," Bliss explained to me. "We call him Buzzy, but his real name's Sebastian." She turned her attention back to Buzzy, rubbing her nose to his. "Were you sleeping?" She kissed him on the cheek as she carried him over to the chair and sat down with him on her lap. Buzzy looked at me warily, not sure what to make of me. The feeling was mutual; I never knew how to behave around little kids.

Buzzy wiggled out of Bliss's lap and ran into the garden giggling. I watched the scene and felt bad that I had been so judgmental earlier. Observing Bliss's family created a sense of serenity inside of me, but I also felt jealous.

I looked at David again. He was still sitting on the bench with his face all bunched up. I turned to Bliss. "I need to go. There's something that I said I would do today."

"Do you need some help?" Bliss asked.

I didn't feel comfortable telling her about the agreement between David and me. "No, it's probably best if I do this on my own, but I'll see you tomorrow after school and we'll put our plan into motion," I said.

Bliss gave me that all-knowing wink.

I started to walk through the trailer park when Bliss called out, "Evie, you can walk home by following the creek bed. It's dry right now." She walked me to the makeshift bench and pointed down to the creek. There was no water in it, but I'd heard that it would run fast and high in the winter once the rains started. I made my way down into the creek bed and began my walk toward Art Carter's house.

Chapter 4
Power Tools

It was peaceful as I strolled through the creek bed. I focused on my surroundings. I heard birds chirping, and wildlife seemed to be all around me. The trees hung out over the creek with their branches swaying in the wind as if waving to me and welcoming me. I noticed endless blackberry bushes that climbed up the edges of the creek like snakes creeping out of a pit. I could still see some remnants of berries on the bushes. I was beginning to relax a little and had just been considering picking a couple of berries when David spoke and startled me.

"Do you know what you're going to say?" he demanded.

"To your father? No, not really. ... I mean, what am I supposed to say, 'Hello, Mr. Carter you don't know me, but I can see your dead son'? I don't picture that going over very well, do you?" I spat the words out. I was angry that he had just popped up and then started in on me about seeing his dad.

He sighed. "I know you're right. This isn't going to be easy." He ignored my anger and focused on the task of talking with his dad. He was looking down at his feet. Then he slowly raised his face up, looked at me solemnly, and pleaded, "You're my only hope to reach him, Evie."

I didn't feel so mad anymore; instead I felt bad for him. I sat down on a large boulder in the creek bed, rummaged through my backpack, and pulled a piece of paper and a pen out to write some notes. "Why don't you tell me what you want to say to your father?" I suggested.

David smiled. "Hey, that's a good idea. ... How about a letter?" and he began to dictate a letter to me.

Dear Dad,

I miss you. I want you to know that I now understand about that day when you wouldn't let me pull the boat from the water. I understand why you made me watch it disappear down the river. It was about letting go. Now it's your turn to let go. Please don't be sad anymore.

I love you,
David

I reread it and knew it was the right thing for him to say. I wasn't quite sure how to explain to his father why the letter was in my handwriting, but I knew I had to try to deliver it.

I followed David up the small trail that led from the creek bed to Art Carter's house. My heart began to beat wildly. I felt it pounding beneath my chest, as if it were thumping against my chest bone. My face and hands felt hot and clammy at the same time. I couldn't recall a time

I'd ever felt more nervous or frightened. The path from the creek was overgrown and just as creepy as the front driveway.

Standing outside the house I heard some sort of power tool or saw roaring from somewhere inside. I realized how crazy it was to approach a grieving man who owned power tools!

I knocked on the door, although not very loudly, I must admit. "Well," I said, turning to David, "sounds like he can't hear me knocking over the saw. ... Maybe we should try again later."

"Oh no you don't!" David barked. "Knock again ... louder."

This time I banged harder. While still knocking I heard the saw turn off, then heavy footsteps approaching. I would have run away, but I was so scared, my feet wouldn't move. It was as if they had been cemented there. The door opened with a quick, aggressive *swoosh* that practically knocked me off balance.

In the doorway stood a huge man. He was well over six feet. He had broad shoulders and dirty blond hair. He held a piece of wood in his hands that looked like it could be a leg to a chair. His hands were large and rough, as though they would have felt like sandpaper. I stood there for a moment and stared. I was frightened down to the bone; my gaze was fixated on the piece of wood he held. I thought about how it could be used to knock me out.

When I didn't say anything, Art Carter's eyes narrowed. "What do you want?" he demanded.

"Uh ... uh ... Well ... Mr. Carter, my name is Evie, and my mom and I just moved in down the street, and I now go to school at Turnville School and I'm in the eighth grade just like David would have been and"—I knew I was babbling a mile a minute, but I couldn't seem to stop—"and, well ... my first day, which was yesterday, I saw David and he wanted to write you a letter, only he couldn't because, well, he's a ghost, you see, so I wrote this letter ... well, HE wrote the letter, I mean to say it's my writing, but he told me what to write." I held the letter out in front of me, the paper rattling in my shaking hand. Art Carter didn't take it at first. Then after an agonizing minute of silence that seemed to last forever, he snatched the paper from my hand and crumpled it into a wad without even reading it.

"I don't know what kind of joke you're trying to pull here." He raised his voice. "Maybe some of the local kids put you up to this or something, but you'd better get out of here before I call the police." He threw the crumpled paper on the ground; I stood in a state of shock for a moment. When I didn't move, he exploded, "Go on. I said GET!" My heart was racing and I could hardly breathe. I took off and ran down the driveway.

I looked back over my shoulder and saw David standing right in front of Art Carter, stunned. Then David began to chase after me and yelled for me to come back.

"Evie," David yelled desperately. "He didn't read the note. ... You have to go back, you have to tell him about the boat."

Was he crazy? There was NO way I was going back there! Without thinking I turned backward while still running and cupped my hands around my mouth and yelled to Art Carter, "David says he understands now about the boat ... about letting go. He says it's okay to let go." I turned to run forward again and tripped, falling face-first into the gravel. I scraped the palms of my hands. I noticed some blood, but I scrambled to my feet quickly. With my heart ringing in my ears I ran as fast as I could all the way home.

Once my house was in view, I slowed down to a walk and tried to catch my breath. My mother was on the front deck sweeping up redwood needles. I must have looked frightened, because as I walked up the three steps onto the deck, my mom asked, "What's wrong, honey?"

"Nothing," I answered, still breathing heavily. I certainly didn't want to explain what had just happened. I didn't even want to think about it.

I passed my mother, but just as I reached our front door, a large blue Ford pickup pulled up in front of our house. It was Art Carter! He was climbing out of the truck so fast that he was slamming the door of the pickup before the engine was even completely turned off. Why had I told him that we'd just moved in down the street? That was so stupid of me!

He marched up to our house. My mom stopped sweeping and leaned on the handle of the broom. I moved so that I stood behind her. The frightened feeling from earlier crept up my spine again.

My mother opened her mouth to speak, but before she could say anything, Art Carter pointed at me and said, "Keep her away from me!" My mother looked confused.

He continued, "I don't need her coming around and dredging up all this pain and bringing up the past by telling me that she sees my dead boy David." At the mention of David's name my mother seemed to understand from our conversation in the car.

I expected her to turn around and lay into me. I pictured the two of them ganging up on me. Instead she took a deep breath and faced Art Carter squarely, then calmly replied, "No, it seems to me, that you'd rather wallow in your own self-pity over the loss of your son. I'm sure Evie meant no harm." You could have blown me over with a whisper at that moment.

It was a showdown. They stood and stared at each other. Neither one of them moved. Then Art Carter's eyes softened just a tad; it was barely noticeable. I could have sworn there was even a sort of half smile on his face. I had the distinct feeling that he was impressed that my mom had stood up to him. Then he turned on his heels and said over his shoulder, "Just keep her away from me!" We watched him get into the truck and drive away.

When the truck was far enough down the road, my mother briskly turned and faced me. Her face was bright red and her head shook as she yelled, "What on earth were you thinking, Evie? You need to stop all this nonsense about seeing a ghost! What a cruel, cruel thing to do, pulling that man's hurt and grief into your own. I know you're hurting over losing Nonno and leaving your old friends, but stop trying to alienate us from this community. We're here to stay, do you hear me?" She didn't wait for an answer; she threw the broom down on the deck, strode past me into the house, and slammed the front door, leaving me on the deck alone. Her last words, *do you hear me?*, seemed to ring in my ears and resound in the redwood trees all around me.

Chapter 5
New Territory

I didn't see David in school the following day; I figured he was still upset about how everything had gone down between his dad and me.

Bliss was in the other eighth-grade class, so I rarely saw her during class time. However, this day would be different; we received our "book buddies." Once a week the entire eighth grade went to the library and met with all the kindergartners, so I saw Bliss there.

We were assigned a book buddy, a kindergartner to whom we were to read or were to help read to us. I didn't know how to handle younger children, and I dreaded the whole idea of this book buddy thing.

In the library we were paired with our buddies. Ms. Roberts pointed out a little girl, Elizabeth, who was sitting away from the rest of the kindergartners. She appeared withdrawn and timid, her arms drawn in close to her body. She had short blond hair and almond-shaped blue eyes, and her head looked too big for her little body. She didn't fidget like the other kindergartners, but held herself still.

I looked across the library at Bliss with her book buddy. It amazed me how good Bliss was with younger children. She knew how to talk to them. She and her book buddy were giggling and appeared to be having fun.

I took in a deep breath and walked over to Elizabeth.

"Hello, Elizabeth," I said, trying to sound friendly with a forced smile. "I'm Evie, your book buddy. … Um … what book would you like to read?"

"Doesn't matter," she said, looking down at the table in front of her.

I grabbed the closest book within my reach from a nearby bookshelf. "Okay, how about this one?" I looked at the title. "*Matilda?*"

Her almond eyes widened, and she looked up at me with surprise. "That book's too hard. … It's ... it's too big," she replied.

I realized I hadn't any clue what an appropriate book for a kindergartner would be. We finally settled on a Berenstain Bear book. As I read it to her, she didn't seem to be paying attention to me. I felt like a failure, and I was exhausted by the end of the book.

I lamely patted Elizabeth on the shoulder and said, "Goodbye, Elizabeth," then turned to leave. Before I could walk away, Elizabeth grabbed my hand, pulled me closer to her, forcing me to bend over, then whispered in my ear, "Lizzy … please call me Lizzy."

"Is that what everyone calls you?" I asked.

She shook her head and said softly, "No, not everyone. … Just some people, special people."

"Okay, Lizzy," I said, smiling. "I'll see you next week." Maybe I hadn't been quite the failure that I thought I'd been; after all she wanted *me* to call her Lizzy, something she reserved only for special people.

I turned toward the door to line up with my class and saw Bliss giving her book buddy a hug. Interaction with little kids came naturally for her, and I felt another twinge of jealousy. I shook it off and reminded myself that she had a little brother, so she was used to this kind of thing.

After school Bliss and I walked through town to the police station. The police station and courthouse were in the same building. Two patrol cars were parked in front: not much was happening on the crime front in Turnville. As Bliss and I walked up the ten or so steps to the entrance, we passed two lawyers and a police officer leaning against the handrail talking.

We approached the front counter, where an overweight, balding officer sat at a desk drinking a cup of coffee. He didn't see us until Bliss rang the bell at the counter.

The officer looked up. "Well, hello, Bliss," he said as he stood and walked over to the counter. "How're your folks doin'?"

"Oh, they're fine, Ernie," she answered. This was definitely an "everybody knows everybody" kind of town. There was an uncomfortable silence as Bliss didn't offer any more information about her family. It made me think she was hiding something.

"Who's your friend?" Ernie asked in a jovial tone.

Bliss introduced me. He put out his hand. "Nice to meet ya, Evie." When I shook his hand, it felt plump and soft, like uncooked sausages. When he smiled, his cheeks extended out like two red balloons. He reminded me of Santa Claus without the beard. Only later did I learn that

Ernie dressed up as Santa every year for the annual town Christmas celebration.

Ernie remained cheerful. "What can I do for you ladies today?" I looked at Bliss for some guidance. I felt nervous asking for a police report.

Bliss didn't hesitate. "Ernie, can we get a copy of the police report from when David Carter was killed?"

The cheerful expression on Ernie's face dropped. "What do you want with that information?"

"We just want to look at it.... Maybe there's something that got overlooked," she replied. Again, I was astonished at how bold Bliss was; she just seemed more adult than most kids.

"We did a thorough investigation," Ernie said defensively, "and it seems to me that you're digging into things that really don't concern you ... things that might be a bit hurtful to others and better left alone." On his last comment his eyes shifted to me. I wondered if he knew that I had approached Art Carter. I remembered how David's dad had yelled that he would call the police. Had he? Bliss knew nothing about my exchange with Art Carter.

I heard Bliss let out a sigh of resignation. With my thoughts focused on the previous day and how I had run away like a coward, I looked up to see Ernie staring at me accusingly. I felt a surge of courage run straight through me like a lightning bolt. I threw my shoulders back and spoke up in my best businesslike tone. "It IS public record, isn't it? And if we are requesting a copy of it, isn't it your obligation to provide it?" I asked. There was silence for a moment as Ernie and I stared at each other. I hoped I appeared a lot braver than I felt. My knees trembled.

Ernie's eyes narrowed. "I suppose," he said slowly. Then to Bliss he said, "Maybe you can help your new friend understand small-town politeness. This isn't the big city like she must be used to." He didn't wait for a reply; instead he turned abruptly and strode into a back room. Bliss and I gave each other the raised-eyebrow look. We could see him through the doorway and watched as he riffled through file drawers in a cabinet. After a couple of minutes he took out a file, then walked over to a copy machine. He returned to us and held out a copy of the report.

I reached out and grabbed it, but he didn't let go. I was trying to pull it out of Ernie's hand when he warned, "You'd better be careful. I don't want any calls coming here to the station about you two being where you don't belong. ... Do you catch my drift?" Bliss and I both nodded. He let go of the report. Then we hightailed it out of there. I got the feeling that just maybe Ernie knew more about this case than he was letting on.

We rushed across the street to a bench and sat down. We placed the police report between us, leaned our heads in together, and started reading.

The report stated that the incident involving David had been a hit-and-run. The vehicle had been identified as a newer white sedan probably traveling around forty or fifty miles an hour based on measurement of the tire skid marks. Witnesses said the vehicle didn't stop after hitting the victim. Although there had been numerous witnesses, mostly parents dropping off children at the time, no one was able to get a license plate number. The victim was thrown more than thirty feet and died instantly on impact from severe head trauma.

It was odd reading about David as a victim, and it was the first time that his death had a sense of reality to it.

"Wow! I really flew in the air thirty feet?" I jumped at hearing David's voice. He was standing behind us, reading over our shoulders.

Bliss asked, "David, huh?"

"Mmm hmm," I nodded. "He sneaks up without warning a lot!" I threw David a glare to let him know it was annoying.

Bliss spoke very matter-of-factly. "There doesn't seem to be a lot of new information to work with, but at least we know the white car was a sedan and that it's a newer model, so we're probably looking for a car about three or four years old."

Chapter 6
Counting Cars

The next few days we were on the lookout for white cars. We looked as we walked to school. We searched the grocery store parking lot. We sat on the bench downtown and observed cars driving by every day after school. We never saw any white cars ...not a one. It wasn't until Friday after school that we hit the jackpot—the school parking lot.

We never passed through the school parking lot because it was behind the school. We always left through the front of the school toward town.

After school, I stood outside my classroom door waiting for Bliss so we could walk home together.

"Evie," I heard Ms. Roberts call from inside the classroom, "can you help me carry a few things to my car?"

"Sure," I answered as I entered the room. She pointed out a box full of papers for me to carry. I snatched up the box and followed her to the parking lot. She was carrying two other boxes while still holding her keys.

I heard footsteps run up behind us. "Would you like some help with those?" Bliss asked Ms. Roberts.

"That would be great," Ms. Roberts said, sighing while shifting one of the boxes for Bliss to grab.

Bliss and I were walking side by side when I felt Bliss elbow me so sharply in the ribs that I almost dropped the box. I looked over at her and saw that her eyes were as big and round as a zombie's. She jerked her head sideways trying to get my attention. At first I couldn't figure out what she wanted me to look at. It wasn't until I heard Ms. Roberts's keys jingling as she searched to find her trunk key that I noticed we were standing in front of a white Ford Taurus sedan.

Ms. Roberts popped open the trunk. "Thank you, girls, you really saved me from going back and forth." She took the boxes out of our arms and loaded them into her car.

"No problem, Ms. Roberts," Bliss replied.

Ms. Roberts closed the trunk, then walked around to the driver's door. Bliss and I followed. "This sure is a nice car you have here," Bliss said.

"Thank you, Bliss," Ms. Roberts said. She quickly turned her back to us to climb into her car before we could ask her anything more. We heard the car start, so we took a couple of steps back. While Ms. Roberts backed the car out of the parking space, she rolled down her window. "You girls have a nice weekend ... and stay out of trouble." She said it with such a friendly smile that it was difficult to see her as a murderer. Yet no doubt about it, she was now our prime suspect.

We stood there watching her drive out of the parking lot. When her car was out of sight, we began talking a mile a minute over each other.

"What was with the stay-out-of-trouble comment?" Bliss asked.

"You think that was a warning?" I asked, finding that hard to believe. Bliss didn't answer me, but stood frozen, staring. I turned my gaze in the direction that she was looking, and there it was ... another white sedan in the school parking lot. Who did it belong to? We decided to sit down on the log at the edge of the parking lot to wait and find out.

For the first ten minutes Bliss and I chatted about Ms. Roberts and tried to guess who this other car might belong to. Fifteen minutes went by and we began to pick up gravel from the parking lot and toss it at one big stone that stuck out like a sore thumb. It felt nice to sit there with Bliss, saying nothing and tossing rocks. The really nice part about it was that I didn't feel like I *had* to say anything. It was a comfortable feeling that I couldn't recall ever feeling with any of my old friends. With my friends from Oceanside we were always trying to fill the empty spaces with conversation, and as I thought about it, I realized the conversation hadn't always been so nice. ... It had been gossipy.

"Hey, where have you guys been?" I jumped and let out a little yelp when I heard David speak. It seemed to cut into the silence abruptly.

"Does David ever *not* startle you?" Bliss responded to my reaction. "I would think you'd be used to him popping up by now."

"You can't even see him, so you don't know what this is like having him appear when I least expect it," I replied.

"Who does she think she is, my keeper?" David asked, pointing at Bliss.

"My, aren't you snappy?" I said to David, but Bliss was the one to answer.

"I wasn't trying to be snappy!" she remarked.

"No ... ugh ... I hate this," I said, realizing how difficult it was to always be the middle echo. "I was talking to David, not you. ... He was the one that made a snide remark."

"Snide?" David grunted. "I think I have a right to feel 'snappy,' as you call it. I was waiting for the two of you along the usual walk home after school and you didn't show."

With a wicked grin and a bit of sarcasm I replied, "Aww, what a shame that you had to wait so long, but you might be interested to know that we found not just one, but two white cars!"

David looked across the parking lot and a smile stretched across his face. I realized as I watched him that I hadn't really seen him smile like that since the first day of school when he had first discovered that I could see him. "Cool!" he whispered. "Where's the second car?" I filled him in on Ms. Roberts.

I felt Bliss nudge me with her elbow. "Evie, look!" In the parking lot were Nurse Jillian and Mrs. Piper, the principal, walking together toward the only two cars left in the lot. Could the white car be Nurse Jillian's? It seemed unfair. I had met only two staff members here at Turnville School, Ms. Roberts and Nurse Jillian. They both had been so nice to me. Were they both going to turn out to be our main suspects?

The principal and Nurse Jillian stopped in the parking lot and finished their conversation, and then they split up to go to their cars. I was relieved when it was Mrs. Piper who walked over to the white car. She saw us sitting on the log at the edge of the parking lot and waved to us. With our mouths hanging open, we waved back.

We watched them drive away, leaving the parking lot deserted except for the three of us. We all got up and walked home. We were silent at first, each of us digesting the idea that Ms. Roberts or Mrs. Piper might be responsible for David's death. It just didn't seem possible, yet they were our only two suspects, and the fact that they worked at the school, where the hit-and-run had happened, made them likely suspects.

"You know," Bliss said, breaking the silence, "we're going to have to find a way to question Ms. Roberts and Mrs. Piper. ..." Her thought trailed off. She was right, but how?

As we approached the creek bed, David said he would see us later and disappeared. I figured he was going to check in on his dad. He never brought up what had happened that day with his dad, and I was glad of it too, because I didn't want to go through that again! When David was gone, I wanted to tell Bliss about Art Carter, but for some reason I thought that if I did, I would be betraying David's trust. I don't know why I felt that way; he had never asked me not to tell Bliss.

Bliss and I continued the silent walk down the creek bed. When we neared the trailer park, I asked her what she was doing over the weekend.

She had no plans, so I invited her to come over to my house on Saturday. She thought that was a great idea and said we should both work on ideas on how we could interview Ms. Roberts and Mrs. Piper, then discuss them on Saturday. She ran up the side of the creek bed to the trailer park, turned around, and waved goodbye.

I continued my stroll home along the creek bed. I enjoyed having a brief moment to myself under the trees.

Watching the waving trees my thoughts turned to Bliss: how homely she looked, and how pretty she would be if she would just wear something more stylish and take her hair out of that braid she wore all the time. She was smaller than me, and I knew I still had some old clothes from the previous year that I had outgrown that would probably fit her perfectly. I resolved that when I arrived home, I would go through my clothes, and then on Saturday I would give her an "Evie Special Makeover"—at least that's what my old friends used to call it.

I walked up from the creek bed onto Cherry Lane and approached my house. I was unprepared for what lay waiting for me on the deck.

Sitting in the most beautiful wooden rocking chair I had ever seen was my mother. She was still wearing her business suit, and she rocked slowly back and forth. Her briefcase lay on its side next to the chair while she rubbed her hands on the chair's arms with such care it was as if she was caressing the smooth wood. She traced the carved designs in the arms with her fingers.

She looked up at me surprised; she hadn't realized I had been standing there. She stopped rocking as if embarrassed that I had caught her in such an unguarded moment. "I came home and found these on the deck," she said.

These? I thought. She must have caught my bewildered look, because she motioned to the picnic table behind her. Then I noticed it. … I held my breath, and it felt as though my heart skipped a beat. On the picnic table was the most elaborate and intricate model sailboat that I'd ever seen.

"Where …?" I asked

"I don't know for sure, but I have an idea," she said.

Of course I had the same idea. "Was there a … a note or anything?" I asked.

"No. I just got home from work and here they were on the deck. Perhaps they're a truce, maybe some kind of offering of peace. They're such beautiful pieces, don't you think?" She touched the arm of the chair again.

I didn't know what to think of the boat. What did he mean by giving it to me? Did Art Carter believe me about David? Was it really a gift, or was it supposed to make me feel guilty for the whole exchange we'd had?

I walked up to the boat, putting my face close to it but still too afraid to touch it. The details were amazing. A fine wire attached the sails to the beams. The railing that encircled the rim of the boat was as thin as a toothpick. The sails were actually made of canvas, and there was a crow's nest at the top of the center mast. The wood was a cherry color with a polished shine to it.

I thought back to the story that David had told me, about when he had had to let go of the boat and watch it float down the river. Was his boat *this* beautiful? If it was, I now understood why letting go of it was so difficult. I finally let out my breath, unable to hold it in any longer. As I released the air, I could see the sails move slightly, as if flapping in a breeze.

Chapter 7
A Day of Discovery

Saturday morning I wanted to sleep in, but the sun crept into my room through a crack in the curtains, taunting me and beckoning me to open them. I couldn't force myself back to sleep, and that sliver of sun took over the room like an uninvited guest. I lingered in bed and watched the dust particles float in the sun's rays, and then I looked over at my dresser where the sailboat sat. I still felt confused about it.

I rolled out of bed onto my feet and shuffled into the kitchen. My mother was hunched over at the kitchen table with a wash towel thrown over her shoulder. Her elbows were propped up on the table with her head between her hands, she took in a deep breath. On the table was a stack of bills. Once she realized I had entered the room, her demeanor changed and she pretended to be light and airy. She tossed the towel on top of the papers and envelopes. "Good morning, sweetie," she said. "Would you like some waffles?"

"Nah, I'll just make myself some toast. ... Bliss is coming over today."

"That's great," she said. "I'm glad you're starting to make some friends here."

When she said that, I wanted to shout at her, "Yeah, but she's not like my friends back at Oceanside—Bliss is a geek!" but at the same time I knew that I really liked Bliss because she *was* different from my old friends.

After breakfast I returned to my room and hid the sailboat in my closet. I didn't know how I was going to explain it to Bliss. I didn't even know how I was going to tell David about it ... or *if* I was going to tell him.

I placed the stack of my old clothes that I'd sorted through the previous evening on the bed ready for the makeover with Bliss. I showered and got dressed, and Bliss arrived shortly afterward.

Bliss was frustratingly friendly with my mom right away, acting as if she had always known her. I could tell my mom liked her right off the bat too. I grabbed Bliss's hand and dragged her from the kitchen into my room.

Bliss noticed the pile of clothes on my bed. She looked at the clothes and then at me with a questioning look. All of a sudden I wasn't sure how to approach the subject. I didn't want to hurt her feelings. I said, "Yesterday I was going through some of my old clothes that don't fit anymore."

"Oh," Bliss said quietly.

Hurriedly I went on, "It's just that ... uh ... I ... well, you're smaller than me, and I thought that maybe you'd want to go through them and see if there's anything you want." This was not going the way I had planned it in my mind. I had imagined that we were going to put on makeup, giggle, and do "girly" stuff like my old friends and I used to do. Maybe I would teach her something about fashion and she'd be grateful. Instead the whole thing felt awkward. I had the impression Bliss was hurt by the suggestion, and I felt like an awful friend.

We stood in silence for a moment. I quickly appraised Bliss as she stood there. She had on a long, faded denim skirt and tie-dye T-shirt. She wore a small beaded purse over her shoulder. Also hanging off her shoulder was a water bottle attached to a string-like strap. As unstylish as she was, she had a style all her own that I really did admire. Maybe it wasn't the style so much as it was that she just didn't seem to care what others thought about her.

Bliss finally broke the uncomfortable quiet and said, "You know, that's real nice, and I could use some new clothes, but you don't mind if maybe we go through them later, do you?" I shrugged in response, pretending like it was no big deal.

She continued, "It's just that it's such a beautiful, sunny, warm day today and I thought we could do some exploring outside. ... It feels like summer!" She had that already familiar mischievous look.

On the deck I felt relieved to be out of the house. Bliss was right, it was just like summer! The majestic redwoods reached up into the sunshine, I could see streams of light pouring down through the branches, and there was a smell like ... well, like summer. Nothing else describes that scent. It's fresh and stale at the same time. It's a smell that makes you feel like time is standing still. I was also glad that I didn't have to worry about Bliss stumbling onto the sailboat in my closet.

We walked down Cherry Lane toward River Road while talking about how we could go about interviewing Mrs. Piper and Ms. Roberts, but the conversation didn't get very far because neither one of us had any idea what we could do. I kept expecting David to pop up and join in on the conversation, but he didn't and I was glad for it. I was truly enjoying the weather; it was the first time since we had moved to Turnville that I actually felt relaxed.

"I noticed your dad wasn't at your house," Bliss said. "Are your parents divorced?"

It seemed like a nosy question, but then, Bliss was a straightforward person. "No," I answered. "I never really knew my father. He died before I was even a year old."

"How'd he die?"

"Car accident," I said, and I relayed the story of my father's death the same way I always did. "It was late at night and it was raining pretty hard. His car slid into the opposite lane with oncoming traffic and another car hit him head-on."

"Oh, I'm sorry," Bliss said.

"I don't remember any of it." I could tell Bliss felt bad about bringing it up, so I said, "You're lucky to have your dad around. I mean, I'd like to know what it's like to have a father and all, but since I've never really had one ... I guess I don't know what I'm missing." I knew it was a lie as I said it. My Nonno had been just like a father, and I missed him with every fiber of my being. I knew *exactly* what I was missing.

I missed Nonno's gentle arm around my shoulder as we walked to the beach, I missed our shared secrets, I missed sitting on the pier and listening to his stories, I missed his laugh that sounded like a crow cackling quickly, I missed how we would people-watch together and then make up stories about the people we saw, I missed sharing a bowl of popcorn and watching old movies together. He was the only other person who liked what we called "spicy corn" where we'd sprinkle a little Tabasco sauce on our popcorn. Oh, I missed him terribly!

I didn't want to tell Bliss about Nonno. Maybe I wasn't ready to talk about it. I was afraid I'd break down and start crying. It was easier to let her think I'd never had a father. … After all, Nonno had been my grandfather.

Bliss veered from the road slightly onto a neighbor's small lawn and picked two bright yellow dandelions. She handed one to me.

"You know," she said, "dandelions are edible." Then she popped hers in her mouth and ate it, acting like it was the most ordinary thing to do. I looked down at the dandelion in my hand, twirling the stem between my fingers. I'd only ever thought of them as bothersome weeds. Then, not knowing what to expect, I followed her lead and popped it in my mouth and chewed it. It was bitter, and it felt odd rolling around in my mouth. The petals were soft and squishy, yet it seemed exotic to be eating a flower.

"There are all sorts of edible flowers," Bliss said as she chomped on her dandelion, "like marigolds, … They're my favorites. Sometimes my mom will even put marigolds in our salad. Nasturtiums are tasty too; they have a spicy, peppery flavor."

"I don't think I have ever eaten flowers before," I said.

"What about honeysuckles? You have to have had honeysuckles. Every kid has had honeysuckles."

I shook my head.

"Well, that's just a shame! I'll keep my eyes out for some, although it's really not the right season."

When we approached River Road, I thought we would turn left and head toward town, but instead Bliss led me across the road down a small dirt lane.

"Where are we going?" I inquired.

"The river."

I hadn't really thought about it until that moment, but I had yet to see the river. Of course I'd seen it from the road and passed it all the time on the way to school, but I hadn't actually been up to the water's edge. It seemed ironic in a way because the river was such an important part of the town. Turnville got its name because it's at the largest turn in the river. Some people in town have said that the turn is the town's greatest nemesis—it's what's caused the town to flood in heavy rain years. During science, Ms. Roberts had even made reference to how it could become an oxbow lake someday.

Not very far down the dirt lane we turned off to go down an old, overgrown dirt driveway. I could see a boarded-up house at the end. It was odd, but the house wasn't spooky or creepy like Art Carter's house was. The thought occurred to me that here was a house that had been abandoned and no one lived in, yet it seemed friendlier than a house where a person actually resided.

Bliss circled around the house to the backyard. I followed. She walked up to some bush-like plants. She picked the flowers and put them in her beaded purse. Then she took the water bottle she had been carrying and poured the water over the base of the plants.

"What is this place?" I asked while looking around.

"It's where I used to ... Well ... this used to be my house," she replied. "This is all that's left of my mom's old herb garden ... some lavender and rosemary. Here, smell."

She reached out, broke a piece off one of the plants, and handed it to me. I recognized the scent of lavender at once. She continued to tend to the plants with care.

"I try to come and give them water." She stood up, then broke off some more of the flowers and slipped them into her beaded purse too. She walked over to the house. I looked out the other direction, noticing that the house backed up to the same creek that my house was on. It was the first time it struck me that that little creek traveled all the way to the river.

On the deck, Bliss sat on an old porch swing. I followed her and sat down next to her. We swung slowly, rhythmically. I looked at her as she stared out across the overgrown yard.

"What happened?" I asked.

"We were flooded out."

I didn't know what to say. I had so misjudged her living situation. I had assumed that she had always lived in a trailer park, yet there we were sitting on the porch of what was once a beautiful home ... her home.

"The house was too low," Bliss explained. "You know, it was below the flood level, so we couldn't get insurance until we raised the house above the floodplain. My parents were saving up to jack it up higher, but they didn't do it soon enough." She paused a moment, lost in thought. "We still own the property and my parents are hoping that someday we can move back, but we just can't afford to repair the house *and* raise it now. My dad says that we're lucky we still have the property."

My heart sank as she spoke. Bliss had always struck me as such a happy-go-lucky person; her entire family seemed to possess that quality. I would never have imagined that such a tragedy had struck them. We swung together in silence for a while.

I realized I'd started the day with the expectation that I would be teaching Bliss things with my planned makeover, and yet I was the one learning so much. How presumptuous of me!

Bliss got up and walked down to the creek bed, then turned back to me. "C'mon. Let's get down to the river. It's such a great day!"

We followed the creek bed just a short way until it opened up to a small beach at the river. Up close I realized what a big river it really was. We stood at a rather wide section of it. It wasn't one of those types of rivers with large boulders protruding out. Instead the water was smooth all the way across and moved at a steady pace. It had a greenish color to it.

The beach was partially sand and partially rock. We took off our socks and shoes. Bliss had on a skirt, but I had to roll up the bottom of my jeans. We dipped our feet into the water, then picked up rocks and skipped them across the water. Bliss was really good at it. She could get six or seven skips out of a rock, whereas I was lucky to get two or three. I began to feel uncomfortably hot standing in the sun as the heat beat down on us. I was just thinking how refreshing it would be to jump in the river and go for a swim when I looked over and saw Bliss undressing down to her underwear. I was shocked. She ran into the water with a splash.

"Come on!" She waved her arms for me to follow her in.

"Uh ... I don't know, Bliss."

"What? Are you afraid of the water? Or can't you swim?" she teased.

"No, no, it's nothing like that. It's just that ... well, I don't have my swimsuit and ... and," I stammered.

Bliss yelled out across the water, "You don't need a swimsuit. Besides, your underwear and bra are just like a swimsuit." She splashed water toward me. "Come on. Who's around to see?"

The water looked inviting, and the more I watched her swim around, kicking in the water, the more tempting it became. I glanced around in all directions, but there wasn't anyone around. There weren't even any houses this close to the river. Bliss's old house was the closest house in the area, and it was still up the creek a ways.

I slid off my jeans while still on the lookout for anyone. I pulled off my shirt quickly and then crossed my arms in front of me even though I still had on my bra. It felt uncomfortable, but as I thought about all those times I had surfed back in Oceanside, I realized that Bliss was right: my underwear and bra were just like those two-piece bathing suits I wore all the time at the beach. It felt awkward only because I knew I was standing there in my underwear. I walked quickly into the water. Once I submerged myself in the water, I instantly felt refreshed and the embarrassment subsided.

I swam and joined Bliss. I could feel the water moving. It wasn't like the ocean waves that I was used to, but it was still a thrill to be in moving water again. As I neared the middle of the river, I could feel its pull become stronger. Bliss was swimming facing upstream, but not going anywhere. I began to do the same thing. I could feel my muscles working to fight the water's current.

I stopped fighting the current for a moment and rolled over to float on my back. I looked up at the trees that extended into the sky from the river's shore. It was amazing as I floated, feeling the river carry me, not fighting it but feeling part of it. An osprey hawk flew over me as it searched for a tasty trout to snatch up from the river.

After floating a ways, I swam toward shore and out of the current to get back upstream, then swam back into the middle and let the current carry me again. Round and round I went like that, feeling the energy of the flow of the river.

Bliss saw me and soon we were both floating and swimming as though we were on a water carousel ride.

We swam to shore and pulled ourselves up on the beach. We laid our clothes down on the rocks and sand, then sat on them to dry off in the sunshine. I no longer felt self-conscious about wearing just my underwear and bra.

Bliss focused intently on the water in front of us. Without taking her eyes off the water she said, "If you listen carefully, you can hear the river whisper."

"What does it say?" I half snickered.

She ignored my giggle. "Well, it says different things to different people. You have to really clear your mind to hear it. Sometimes it doesn't even talk to you; sometimes you can just overhear it whispering to the ocean, telling the ocean that it's on its way. The ocean is like a big heart and the river is like a vein that feeds into it."

I found her perspective on the relationship between the ocean and the river fascinating and familiar. I recalled sitting at the beach in Oceanside next to Nonno. I remembered that as we listened to the waves crash, Nonno had said something similar. He said that the crashing of the waves seemed to happen with the same rhythm as a heart. Nonno then put his arm around me and we listened. CRASH went the wave, *thump thump* went our hearts. CRASH … *thump thump* … CRASH … *thump thump*.

Bliss stared at the river. I wrapped my arms around my legs and leaned in to try to listen too. At first I didn't hear anything, and then I noticed the wind swishing through the tops of the trees overhead. I looked up and watched the branches move in the light breeze. Bliss must have noticed that I was looking up at the trees, because she said, "Oh yes, the wind and trees talk too, but the river … It's harder to hear because it doesn't yell like the wind. … It whispers, so you have to listen carefully."

I stared out across the river again, watching its movement, trying hard to clear my mind of all that had happened over the last few weeks. I focused on watching the water's movement, and then an idea began to form in my head. It was fuzzy at first like the coastal fog, but then the idea began to grow and get clearer, as if the fog was burning off. There was an overwhelming sensation that felt as if the river was whispering this idea to me. It had to be the river, because I certainly couldn't come up with such a harebrained idea all on my own, and it was crazy! There was no possible way that I would ever follow through on this new idea that was formulating in my brain because it would mean having to face Art Carter again. Forget that! Yet the whisper kept nagging at me as I sat there.

Just as I was wrapping my brain around this ludicrous idea and all its implications, there was a rustle in the brush behind us.

Both Bliss and I jumped up. I grabbed my clothes and held them in front of me. Out of the bushes leaped the

Piper twins, Jake and Johnny. At first they didn't notice us because they were lunging toward each other and swinging sticks at each other as if they were in a sword fight. Together, they turned at the same moment. They stopped instantly with sticks still frozen in midair. And the four of us stood face to face. They instantly sized up the situation, with Bliss and I standing there in our underwear trying to hide ourselves with our clothes.

"What do we have here?" Jake said, drawing out each word slowly.

"Turn around right now!" demanded Bliss. Johnny turned his back right away, but Jake stood there staring a moment until Johnny hit Jake in the arm and then Jake turned around. Bliss and I quickly put our clothes on. I saw Johnny glance over his shoulder briefly at me, but I just glared at him.

Johnny and Jake didn't look anything alike; they were fraternal twins. Jake was short, skinny, and wiry, with buzzed, short whitish blond hair. Johnny was tall, wide, and clumsy, with darker, longer dirty blond hair. Their personalities were opposite too. Jake was known to cause trouble when the opportunity arose. ... He had a mean streak in him. Johnny was calmer, quieter, and always seemed like he was thinking or planning something.

Jake was in Bliss's class and Johnny was in mine. Even though Johnny sat right in front of me in class, I never talked to him, mostly because I was embarrassed. He had been the one who had helped carry me down the hall that first day of school.

Once we were dressed, Bliss addressed Jake. "You had better not say a thing about this at school or I'll tell your aunt about how you were trying to sell that pack of cigarettes to a group of fourth graders before school the other day."

"Hey, hey, now," Jake said in an annoying tone. "No need to be like that. I'm not going to tell. Besides, there's nothing to tell. ... I mean, c'mon, Bliss, there was *nothing* to see." Bliss narrowed her eyes. If I hadn't known Bliss better, I'd have thought she was going to punch Jake on the spot. Johnny stood there, quiet as usual, and doing nothing to alleviate the awkwardness of it all.

Jake turned his attention to me. "Aah, it's the town ghost buster, right? I mean, that's what people are saying, at least." It had never occurred to me that I might be part of the town's gossip, but when Jake said that, I recalled some of the strange looks I had received when I was at the grocery store with my mom.

"What exactly are they saying?" I asked warily.

"That you talk to yourself, that you've been nosing around into David Carter's death, getting copies of police reports, stuff like that." At the mention of his name, David appeared as if on cue behind Jake.

"Oh brother," David said, rolling his eyes.

My gaze must have shifted a bit to where David was because Jake's sarcasm increased. "What, Evie, is David here now?" Jake walked in a circling motion with his arms out, swinging his stick around. "Is he haunting us? What does he have to say? Come out, come out, wherever you are." Jake chuckled a mean laugh that emanated from his throat.

David responded, "Geez, Jake, you really still are Jakey the Jerk!"

I didn't like Jake taunting me. I took a deep breath and confronted him. "Yeah, as a matter of fact he is here right now and he says you're a big fat jerk!"

"Oooh, he does, does he?" Jake said, smirking.

"No, no, no, Evie," David said. "Call him Jakey the Jerk."

"Wait a minute," I said. "He's telling me I got it wrong. I didn't say it right. What he actually said was that you're still Jakey the Jerk!" Jake's grin disappeared instantly, and he turned pale. I could tell he was struggling to get his composure back. He glanced around. Even Johnny looked a little shaken and surprised.

"Well, who needs you girls anyway," Jake said, turning to Johnny. "Come on. We came here to swim, not gab with a couple of dumb girls." He pulled off his T-shirt and ran into the water with his cutoffs on. "Come on, Johnny, are you coming or what?"

Johnny didn't move for a moment. Instead he looked me straight in the eyes while biting down on his lower lip. He nodded absently as if answering his brother. His eyes were warm, and his cheeks appeared soft and pink. I had a strange desire to touch his cheek, but he broke our gaze, took off his T-shirt, and ran into the river too. Bliss grabbed my hand and pulled me away.

Bliss, David, and I started our journey back up the creek bed. I turned back just once to see Johnny standing waist high in the water looking back at me.

"Hey, Bliss," I asked, "what did you mean when you told Jake that you would tell his aunt on him?"

"Oh, it's just that their aunt is the principal." As the words came out, she stopped walking and hit her palm to her forehead. "Of course! How stupid of me ... Their aunt is THE PRINCIPAL!" That's when we mapped out a plan to find out about Mrs. Piper's white car.

As we sorted out our scheme, I secretly looked forward to it, because it meant that we would need to talk to Johnny Piper again.

There was still another plan whirling around in my head at the same time. A secret plan known only to me, whispered to me by the river. I was still sorting through it, and even though it was an insane plan ... I thought it just might work.

Chapter 8
A Sea Story

In class Monday, I was too embarrassed to look up from my desk. I could feel Johnny's eyes on me. I could always sense it when he turned around in his seat from time to time to look back at me. My ears would burn, and I pretended not to notice. We had reading buddies again, so the class lined up and marched over to the library.

In the library, Lizzy was waiting for me. She had come prepared, holding a book. I guess she had figured out that I wasn't very good at choosing books. Actually I didn't feel like I was very good at this whole reading buddy thing at all. It was another sunny day, so the teachers and the librarian let those of us who wanted to go outside do so. There was a courtyard area behind the library that was fenced off with two large fruitless mulberry trees.

Lizzy took me by the hand and led me outside. We sat under one of the trees, and she handed me the book she had brought. She held out a book called *The Big, Blue Sea*. It had a picture of an ocean wave crashing onto a sandy beach. I looked at the picture of the ocean and it created a tight pain in my heart as I remembered walking to the pier so many times with my Nonno. As he fished he would share his sea stories with me, and as much as I loved mythology, I loved my grandfather's sea stories most of all.

He had been a fisherman most of his life before he retired and came to live with my mother and me in Oceanside. I had been four years old at the time. He was a real salty old sea dog too—couldn't get the fishing out of him. Most days after school he and I would go to the pier, where he would throw a line in the water and we'd sit on top of the ice chest. While he fished he would tell me his sea stories. They were fascinating, filled with hysterical, lively characters and incredible sea creatures.

I ached for one of his stories at that moment as I stared down at Lizzy's book.

"Evie, aren't you going to read the book?" Lizzy asked.

"Uh ... sure. ... Lizzy, do you like stories about the ocean?" I asked as I held up the book.

"Oh yes," she replied enthusiastically, which was unusual for her. "This book is one of my favorites." Her voice softened. "My sister used to read it to me all the time."

"Your sister?" But she didn't say anything more about it. Instead she placed her hands in her lap and looked down, as if she regretted having said anything. The two of us sat there floundering, not knowing what to do next. I took a deep breath. I needed to be mature about this and set the example.

"Lizzy, why don't we save this book for next time? Instead I know a real sea story. Would you like to hear it?" Lizzy's eyes moved up toward me, but her head remained down. I continued, "It's about a fisherman named

Francisco." Lizzy nodded. I dug deep into my heart. It felt strange using my grandfather's real name for the character of the story, but it was his story, and so I began retelling my favorite of all my Nonno's stories.

"One day while Francisco was far, far out at sea on a large fishing ship with no land in sight, he did what he loved to do most. He stood at the bow of the ship and watched the dolphins swim and dance in the water. Dolphins do that—they like the speed with which the boat propels them along." Lizzy started to show some interest. "Every morning as the ship traveled, Francisco would go to the front of the boat and watch the dolphins glide through the water, and he noticed that one dolphin was always there. Day in and day out that one dolphin never left."

"How did he know it was the same dolphin?" Lizzy asked.

"Well, that was what was so interesting about this particular dolphin. It had a long gash, a scar of some sort, across the top of its head right in front of its spout. The spout on a dolphin is kind of like its nose, and the scar on this dolphin made Francisco think of his wife, Paulina. Paulina had passed away just a few months before, and he missed his wife terribly. They had grown up together on Sicily in a small fishing town."

"But why did the dolphin remind him of his wife?" Lizzy inquired.

I acted like I hadn't heard her question. "Francisco thought Paulina was the most beautiful girl he'd ever known. She had long brown hair that sparkled with a twinge of red in the sunlight, and her smile was so infectious that anyone who saw her smile couldn't help but smile back. Her skin was soft and a lovely dark olive color, but she had one great flaw: a scar across the ridge of her nose that ran up to the top of her head."

I heard Lizzy say, "Mmm, I get it, but how did she get the scar?"

"When Paulina was a little girl, she loved to climb trees. One day while Francisco was working in the olive orchard, Paulina had climbed a nearby tree. From the corner of his eye, Francisco could see the branch that Paulina was sitting on snap. She began to fall, and without thinking, Francisco hopped off the ladder he was on and threw himself under the tree to break Paulina's fall. Many who saw him said that she would have broken her neck had Francisco not saved her. However, when Paulina fell, she sliced her face on the branches, and it left a large scar that ran from the ridge of her nose to the top of her head.

Francisco looked over the side of the boat and began talking to the dolphin, which he had named Paulina because of the scar. 'Ah, Paulina,' he said, 'I have missed you. You must miss me too, to keep coming to my ship and visiting me like this every day.' So every morning he went to the front and every day Paulina was there riding the waves. Francisco tried to tell the other sailors that the same dolphin traveled daily with their ship. They had heard him calling it Paulina and teased him, saying that he was so heartsick for his wife that he was now in love with a dolphin. Francisco smiled and let them give him a bad time, but it didn't stop him from talking to Paulina.

"One morning he went out to greet Paulina as he did every morning, but on this particular day Francisco leaned too far out over the railing and fell into the ocean." I paused to see if Lizzy was still interested, a lot like my Nonno did when he told me a story.

Lizzy asked, "What happened? Did someone save him?"

"No, nobody on the ship saw him fall overboard, so they didn't even know he was missing. He banged his head on the side of the ship as he landed in the water. He went swirling deeper and deeper into the dark ocean. …" I knew I had Lizzy's attention. She had that look that I'd had so many times when my Nonno told this story. I felt like a fisherman myself. … I had Lizzy hook, line, and sinker!

I wasn't expecting it, but it felt really good to be telling Nonno's story. It was the first time I understood that a piece of my Nonno didn't die; part of him continued in the stories that he shared … that I was now sharing.

"Now, Francisco was a strong swimmer, but as the boat pulled away from him, it pushed him deeper down into the swirling water. He tried desperately to swim up to the surface, but he was disoriented and couldn't figure out which way he needed to swim. He knew he couldn't hold his breath much longer. Just as he was thinking that the sea would take him if he didn't get air soon, he saw a large creature in the distance swimming toward him."

"Francisco had often seen twenty-foot great white sharks when he fished far out, and he knew that what was swimming toward him was probably a shark. The thought of being eaten frightened him down to his very bones. As the figure came closer, he could see that he was right: it was a shark! When the creature was just about upon him, Francisco took in a deep swallow of water, as if gasping for air but taking in the water instead. Then he felt the slimy skin of the creature touch him and felt his body jolt with a slam."

Lizzy's hands were curled into fists under her chin. She practically yelled, "Oh no! Was he eaten? Did he drown? Did he die?"

"Evie! Elizabeth!" Someone snapped us out of our story, and we both looked up. "We've been calling for everyone to line up for a couple of minutes now." It was the librarian.

"Sorry," I said. We jumped to our feet. I looked past her into the library and could see that almost everyone else was lined up at the door ready to go.

Lizzy grabbed my hand. "Will you finish your story next time? Will you tell me more?"

I squeezed her hand. "Of course," I reassured her. "I'll definitely tell you what happened to Francisco." I walked her to where the kindergartners were lining up. Lizzy didn't usually smile, but I could see a grin on her face as if she had a secret now ... a secret that belonged to just her and me.

Chapter 9
Change in Plans

At lunch, Bliss, David, and I met before going to the cafeteria. We needed to touch base before following through on our plan. We were going to question Johnny about his aunt. I was a little nervous after what had happened over the weekend, but Bliss had an air of excitement about her.

Just as we anticipated, Jake wasn't with Johnny at lunch because he had to serve a lunch detention with his teacher for acting up in class. It was pretty typical; you could almost always count on Jake getting a lunch detention three or four days out of the week for some smart-aleck remark or not having homework done.

Bliss and I bought our lunches and carried our trays to where Johnny was sitting. He had a sack lunch and was taking out his sandwich when we sat down across from him. He glanced up with a quizzical look, but didn't say anything. We didn't normally sit near him and he seemed aware of that, but he shrugged it off. At first we acted like it was no big deal that we were sitting across from him. Bliss and I carried on a boring conversation, comparing what I was doing in my class versus what she was doing in her class. David quietly sat next to Johnny with anticipation. Every now and then I looked over at David to see what he was doing, and I think Johnny thought I was looking at him. David sat there with his chin propped in his hands like he was watching a movie.

Johnny munched away on his lunch, trying to ignore us. We had planned every part of this conversation; we had even practiced it on the way to school that morning so it wouldn't sound too fake. Bliss brought up Jake being held in detention in her class and looked over at Johnny. "Hey, Johnny, how come you never get in trouble like your brother?" she asked, trying to sound casual.

"Well, I suppose it's because I don't do anything to get in trouble," he said.

"Yeah, you and Jake sure are nothing alike. … How do you put up with him?" she asked.

"He's my brother, I have to," he replied.

Bliss chuckled a little too enthusiastically. "Yeah, I'll bet your aunt sees more of Jake than she would like to here at school, I mean, being principal and all, huh?"

"Probably," he mumbled.

Johnny was keeping his remarks short and to the point. After he'd answer, he'd look over at me and I'd look down at my lunch. I wasn't saying much of anything. I let Bliss do the work because I wanted to stay focused on our plan.

"Speaking of your aunt, Evie and I saw her driving through town the other day. … I didn't realize that she drove a white car." There was no response from Johnny, so Bliss continued, "How long has she had that car? I mean, it seems pretty new." Johnny paused and looked back and forth at the two of us. Bliss acted nonchalant about the question, so I tried to do the same.

He finally answered, "Don't rightly know."

"She's your aunt and you don't know?" Bliss asked as if that were unusual.

"Nope. …" He paused. "Why are you so interested?"

"Oh, no reason … just saw her driving … just curious, I suppose. You know, since she's principal and all, I just figured she'd be driving a different kind of car or something."

Bliss gave me a look and lowered her eyebrows in defeat. The conversation was not going the way we had planned. Either Johnny knew something and wasn't telling or he really didn't know anything like he was claiming. We quickly finished eating, left the cafeteria, and returned to our usual bench outside in the sunshine.

"Well, that was useless," Bliss said.

"Yeah, we'll have to come up with another idea," I said.

David seemed down. "I don't know—maybe we should try Jake."

"No way!" Bliss and I said in unison.

The bell rang and we decided to talk more after school.

On our walk home after school David brought up the idea again about approaching Jake. It seemed hard to believe we would have better success with Jake than we had with Johnny.

"Jake's always wise to stuff like that," Bliss said.

"Maybe we're looking at this the wrong way," I suggested. "Perhaps what we need to do is find a way that it works to Jake's advantage to tell us the information we're seeking. … You know, make it seem like it's his idea."

"Hmm," Bliss said. "You know, if we take the right approach, it could work. I mean, Jake does something only if he thinks he's going to get something out of it ... but what can we make him believe he's getting?"

"That's a tough one, but I do like solving puzzles," David said. I repeated what David said for Bliss's benefit.

Bliss climbed up the side of the creek to her place. "We'll all think on it overnight, okay? I'll see you tomorrow." She waved and disappeared.

David and I continued, but after walking just a little ways down, I saw Johnny Piper sitting on a large boulder at the side of the creek bed, tossing rocks down at the ground. I looked around for his brother, but didn't see Jake anywhere. He stood up and galloped toward me. I stopped dead in my tracks, not sure what to do, while David grinned and put his hands on his hips.

As Johnny got closer, I could feel that sensation again of my ears burning and my heart beating faster. I think Johnny sensed that I was a little apprehensive, so he slowed down as he approached. "Do you mind if I walk you home?"

"Uh, sure," I said.

We walked quietly at first, then Johnny spoke. "So, can you really see David Carter?"

I didn't know what to say. If I said yes I sounded crazy, and if I said no I knew it was a lie, and I didn't like lying. Instead I shrugged.

David spoke. "Come on, Evie, tell him the truth." I ignored him. I didn't want to look stupid in front of Johnny again. "Tell him you can!" David demanded.

Johnny said, "You know, I used to hang out with David now and then. He was an okay guy. We played basketball together sometimes." Johnny chuckled to himself. "He wasn't very good though."

"Hey!" David seemed annoyed. "I beat you a few times!" but Johnny didn't hear him and I continued to ignore him.

Then Johnny said, "I even let him win a few times, so he wouldn't feel too bad, 'cause I liked the guy." I smiled, but David frowned. Johnny continued, lost in a memory. "He wasn't like all the other guys around here. Even though he stunk at basketball, I wanted to keep playing with him 'cause I always liked our conversations on the court. He always had a new and fresh perspective on things ... a different way of looking at stuff. He was smart, too, and while we played basketball, he'd find ways to make mathematical equations out of our game. It helped me a lot to remember math stuff that way." This comment made David smile. "It was strange how you knew what David always used to call Jake."

"What do you mean?" I asked.

"Well, the other day when you said, 'Jakey the Jerk,' well, David was the only one to ever call him that. ... Heck, I think David was the only one *brave* enough to call him that. One time Jake tried to punch David for the comment, but I wouldn't let him. That was the only time I ever stood up to Jake, and he left David alone after that. I mean, I've never really had any reason to stand up to Jake, I just let him do his stupid stuff. I mean, I know it's going to get him in trouble one way or another, so why should I intervene?"

"Where *is* Jake right now?" I asked.

"See—that just proves my point; he got in trouble at home over the weekend, so he's grounded for the rest of the week and had to go straight home from school." I was relieved that Jake wasn't going to be sneaking up on us, and I began to relax with Johnny.

"Evie." Johnny stopped and grabbed me at the forearm. His touch felt warm, and all my focus went to his fingers as they wrapped around my arm. He stooped a little to line our faces up and looked me dead straight in the eyes, just like he had at the beach. I found it difficult to look away. His blue eyes drew me in. "Look, I can tell you want some sort of information about my aunt. Does it have to do with David?"

I didn't want to lie, but I wasn't sure about filling him in on anything either. "Maybe," I said.

"I'll tell you whatever you want to know about my aunt if you can tell me what David used to call me when we played basketball."

I looked at David, but he pretended to ignore me now, looking around and whistling, as if pondering whether to tell me or not. He was getting back at me for ignoring him just moments before. I sighed deeply.

"Come off it," I said toward David.

"Hey now," Johnny said. "I just want to know if you really see him or not. Don't be mad. I'm not trying to trick you or anything."

David continued to ignore me.

"Fine!" I said to Johnny, but looking intently at David. "Yes, I can really see David." David smiled with satisfaction when I said it, as if he had won the argument.

"Well, then, what did he call me?" Johnny asked again. I looked at David.

"Johnny the Joker," David said.

"Johnny the Joker," I repeated, smiling to myself. The name fit, and I could easily imagine David calling Jake "Jakey the jerk" and Johnny "Johnny the Joker."

Johnny seemed satisfied with the answer too. "Okay, so what do you want to know about my aunt?"

Did this mean that Johnny believed me? There was now another person besides Bliss and her mom who didn't think I was crazy. I confided in Johnny that we needed to know about his aunt's car because David had been hit by a white car.

"There's no way it could have been my aunt," he said. "She's had that car only about three months. She bought it over the summer. She bought it when she was in Arizona. She flew to Arizona to visit an old friend and then didn't want to fly back; she wanted to 'drive and take in the scenery,' that's what she said. So, she bought that car in Arizona, then drove back. It would be impossible for it to have been my aunt. She didn't even have that car during the time of David's accident."

I was disappointed when he told me, but sort of relieved too. I mean, it was nice to know that the principal of my new school wasn't responsible for David's death, but that left only Ms. Roberts. I really didn't want to think it was her. I really liked Ms. Roberts, and she was nice. She was a fun teacher; she had a lot of enthusiasm when she taught.

I looked around for David, but he was gone. I supposed that after winning our little spat, then hearing that it couldn't have been Johnny's aunt, he hadn't seen the need to stick around.

In front of my house Johnny unexpectedly took my hand and held it softly in his palm for a moment, looking at me. "You know, Evie, if there's anything I can do to help … I mean with David and all, just let me know, okay?"

"Okay," I said as his eyes drew me in again. Without any warning he leaned in and gave me a kiss on my cheek. It was awkward, but nice at the same time. I think I had actually wanted him to kiss me on the lips, but I liked that he gave me the peck on the cheek. It was sweet, and it showed me what a gentle person he was. Johnny turned away quickly and started to walk up Cherry Lane. I watched him walk away with his already familiar loping walk. Then he turned around and started to walk backward, looking back at me. I was slightly embarrassed that he caught me watching him walk away, but then he hollered out, "Can I walk you home again tomorrow?" I nodded. He smiled and turned around. I smiled.

How was I going to tell Bliss that Johnny knew about David? Did I have to? Did I need to tell Bliss that Johnny was going to walk me home tomorrow, or would he be discreet and wait until after I dropped her off like he had today? I wasn't sure how I was going to handle any of it. The only real thing I knew at that moment was the tingly, warm feeling of that kiss still on my cheek. With the sensation of that kiss lingering, I felt I could tackle just about anything.

With that notion in my head instead of going into my house I walked the other direction down Cherry Lane toward Art Carter's house to follow through on the secret plan that the river had whispered to me.

Chapter 10
Making a Deal

The effects of Johnny's kiss must have been starting to wear off by the time I reached Art Carter's driveway, because as I looked at the spooky trees that hung down around his place, I wasn't so sure about my idea. After my last experience with Art Carter, I was apprehensive about approaching him again. I felt my heart pounding loudly in my chest, and my palms becoming clammy and sweaty, just like before. I walked up to his door and knocked. There were no drills, saws, or other tools running this time. I held on to the hope that maybe he wasn't home, but before I could turn away, the door opened. Art Carter was just as intimidating as last time, his entire body filling the doorway. Yet somehow he seemed different.

He appeared tired, haggard, worn out. He stood slightly bent over as his bloodshot eyes sized me up. There was a sense of resignation about him. He looked at me, but said nothing. He hadn't slammed the door in my face yet, and I took that as a good sign, so I spoke up. "Mr. Carter, I'm here about a job ... a job for you."

He eyed me warily and still remained quiet, but he opened the door wider and motioned for me to enter his house. I crossed the threshold and the moldy, stale smell rushed up my nostrils immediately. The place was dark and dingy, and I internally questioned my decision to enter his house. It seemed unwise to be there; nobody knew I was there. I didn't tell anyone. I had come on a whim.

I stood to the side until he passed me and led me over to a table. I looked around at the mess. He moved newspapers, books, and stacks of old mail from the table to a nearby counter. I sat down. From the table I had the advantage of seeing both the kitchen and the living room.

Dishes were stacked everywhere in the kitchen; every inch of space was cluttered. Cups were overflowing from the sink. In the living room were a couch, a coffee table, and a rocking chair. I recognized the artwork immediately and knew he had made the chair. I thought perhaps he had made the coffee table too. Blankets lay across the couch, giving the appearance that perhaps he slept there often.

Neither one of us said anything about the boat that he had left on the deck for me. I was grateful that he didn't bring it up, because I didn't know what to say. I wanted to thank him, but it didn't seem the right thing to do at that moment.

"Would you like something to drink?" he asked.

"Sure," I replied meekly.

He walked around the long tile counter into the kitchen and opened the refrigerator. From my vantage point I could see there wasn't much in it: some eggs, a carton of milk, a few beers, mustard, mayonnaise, and salad dressing. He grabbed the carton of milk, opened it, and smelled the milk inside. Apparently it had turned sour, because he scrunched up his face and then chucked the milk carton in a nearby garbage can. "How 'bout some water?" he asked.

"That's fine," I said.

He opened the cabinet and to my surprise there were still two clean glasses. I'd been sure there wouldn't be any left, as it seemed that all the glasses were scattered on the counter and in the sink. He took some ice cubes from the freezer, dropped them in the glasses, then walked to the faucet and filled the glasses up. He returned and placed one in front of me and kept one for himself. I thanked him, and he pulled out a chair and sat down in front of me. I could smell a slight lingering scent of alcohol emanating from him.

"So, what's this job?" he asked. I told him about the job and all that it would entail. When I was finished, he leaned back in his chair and fingered his chin, rubbing the scruffy hair that had grown over the last day or two. He finally spoke. "It doesn't sound like there's much money available for this job, based on what you're telling me, and it sounds like a big job."

"Mr. Carter," I said, "my mom is the new bank manager, and I know that if the job came in at the right price, she could get the bank to fund a loan to do the job. It would be a good business deal for her ... setting up some relations with locals and all." Even as I said it I knew I would need to persuade her, but if Art Carter would back me up, I thought that she might do it.

"Well," he said, "I need to go take a look at it; if it's any good, I'll consider it." I smiled. When he saw me grin, he continued, "I'm not promising anything. ... I'm not quite sure I want to start up this line of business again. I'm just saying I'll go take a look."

"That's good enough for me." I extended my hand for a handshake like we were finalizing an agreement. He hesitated, but then took my hand. His hand felt rough like sandpaper, yet it also felt warm too. He looked down at my hand enveloped in his, and I thought I saw a slight smile. He walked me to the door and we said goodbye.

As I walked away from Art Carter's place, I felt like maybe, just maybe, this crazy plan was going to work.

Chapter 11
A New Member in the Gang

While walking to school the next morning I filled Bliss in on what I had learned from Johnny about his aunt. I couldn't keep it from her. After all, we were investigating this together, and she was my best friend. I even told her how David almost didn't help me out.

However, I didn't tell her about the kiss. The kiss belonged only to me. I didn't tell her about my visit to Art Carter's either, although I knew I would need to tell her sooner or later.

In class, I was a little peeved at first when Johnny pretended that nothing had happened the day before. Then I started thinking about it and was sort of relieved. The one thing that I was learning about living in a small town was that people in small towns talk. Even the kids in small towns talk; gossip seemed to be the regular pastime in Turnville, and besides, there was already enough talk going around about me.

As the day went on, every once in a while Johnny would drop his pencil or look in his backpack for something and turn back and give me that smile. My face would flush and

I glanced around, hoping that no one noticed. His smile was reassuring.

The rest of the week Johnny joined Bliss, David, and me on our walk home after school through the creek bed. Thankfully, Bliss acted like it was no big deal that Johnny was walking with us, and before I knew it, both she and I had included him in all the information we had on David's hit-and-run. He was pulled in and wanted to help investigate our only suspect, Ms. Roberts, but even with the extra person, we still didn't know how to get information from her.

The walk home was filled with new feelings for me. After Bliss would pull off to go to her home, Johnny, David, and I would continue on. A little ways down the creek bed Johnny would reach out and casually take my hand. My heart thumped loudly in my chest every time, but I gladly intertwined my fingers with his.

The first time Johnny took my hand, David said, "Sheesh," rolled his eyes, and then disappeared, leaving Johnny and me to walk the rest of the way on our own. After that David started disappearing when Bliss split from the group.

When it was just the two of us, Johnny and I started talking about new things. Things like our favorite colors, favorite foods, hobbies. He told the greatest jokes and made me laugh a lot. I could see why David had called him "Johnny the Joker." Even though we held hands and explored getting to know each other, there weren't any more kisses when he dropped me off at my house, but I was hopeful every day.

Chapter 12
Bad News, Good News

The weather shifted as the weekend approached. It was overcast and cool. Saturday morning I threw on a pair of sweats and my favorite thick pair of socks and headed out to the kitchen for a late breakfast. I found my mom sitting at the table writing out checks for bills.

"Mornin'," I said as I sat down with my bowl of cereal. "How's it going?"

"To be honest, Evie, it's not going as well as I had hoped," she sighed. When she spoke, I realized that she and I hadn't talked much recently and that I didn't know how things were going with her new job at the bank. She had been so excited about this move that I had assumed her job was everything she had expected.

"What do you mean?" I asked.

"I don't want you to worry over my problems."

"Mom, it's just you and me.… Doesn't that make them *our* problems?" I asked.

She nodded and smiled. "You're growing up so fast." She let out a little snort of amusement. "I just can't figure folks out around here. For some reason most of the residents of Turnville don't do a lot of business with the bank. I don't think they do much business with any bank, even the ones in Colton." Colton was the closest thing to a city near us, about a thirty-minute drive up River Road.

"I don't know what they're doing with their money. ... Sometimes I think they're just like a bunch of old-fashioned country folks hiding their cash in mattresses. I can't figure it out. Not many people coming in for loans, business declining. Maybe it's me. Maybe they don't trust a new person, a stranger, to manage their accounts." She paused, and I could tell she didn't want to tell me the next part because her face grimaced, then softened as if she felt sorry for me. "The main office told me that if local business doesn't increase, they might have to shut this branch down."

"They can't do that!" I protested.

"Actually they can, and very likely will," she said, "but the good news is that they're going to keep me on—they said they'll transfer me to another branch. It would mean we would need to move again though."

The words reverberated in my head. Move again? No way! I was finally making friends here. I couldn't imagine saying goodbye to Bliss. Not to mention that finally a boy *I* liked had taken an interest in me; how could I possibly say goodbye to Johnny? Besides, I hadn't figured out who had killed David yet. I wanted to explode and yell at my mom, but she already looked frustrated, and deep down I knew it wasn't her fault.

I dumped my cereal bowl with half my breakfast still in it in the sink and stormed toward my room. Before I could leave the kitchen, my mom grabbed my wrist gently and looked at me. "These things have a way of working out."

"Right," I scoffed, snatching my arm away.

I threw myself on the bed and looked out the window. The weather matched my mood ... dark and gray. My anger swallowed me up. I felt mad all over. I didn't know what else to do and I wanted to do something so I wouldn't have to think about the possibility of moving. I grabbed a book from my bookshelf, tore the big quilt off my bed, wrapped it around myself, then walked with book, quilt, and bad temper outside. On the deck, I curled up on a lounge chair and tried to read under the gray sky.

I tried reading. I had flipped two pages over, but couldn't really recall what I had just read. As I turned the third page over in my book, I was interrupted by the sound of heavy, clomping shoes stepping up onto the deck. I looked up to see Art Carter standing there in work jeans and a flannel jacket. He gave me a curt nod, and then knocked on the front door. Before I could say anything, my mom answered the door.

"Why hello, Mr...?."

"Carter. Good mornin', ma'am," he said. There was an awkward silence hanging over all of us. My mom glanced over at me. I wanted to get up and ask Mr. Carter about what we had spoken about the other day. I assumed that was the reason he had come, but I was frozen. I couldn't move a muscle. I'm sure I looked ridiculous with my mouth hanging open.

My mother was the first to break the silence. "Mr. Carter, I'd like to thank you for the lovely rocker. You do beautiful work. I have been sitting in it and reading every evening." And she had been too. He seemed pleased and gave her a polite nod.

He didn't even turn to look at me but remained focused on my mother. Then he asked her, "Do you have a moment, ma'am?"

"Jackie, please call me Jackie." My mom looked confused, but she opened the door and motioned for him to enter. "I apologize for being so rude. Won't you come in?" As he stepped into the house, my mom glanced over at me as if she thought that I had something to do with this visit.

I had wanted to talk to my mother first about my plan, before Art Carter did, but the opportunity had never come up. Besides, I didn't want to talk to her about it until I'd heard from Art Carter. I wanted to know if he was even going to do the job first. I hadn't expected him to come straight to my mother.

I desperately wanted to burst into the house and listen to every word. Instead I sat up so that I could see through the large picture window. I watched intently from outside.

My mother poured two cups of coffee. They sat at the kitchen table, and I could see Art Carter, mouth moving. Oh! I ached to hear what he was saying. He appeared very businesslike and matter-of-fact while talking. I strained my ears, trying with all my might to make out any words, but could hear nothing through the thick glass. I even tried to read lips with no success. My mom looked out the window and made direct eye contact with me, and I could make out the one word she said with a questioning look: "Evie?" I realized I was holding my breath. She turned back to Art Carter, and they continued their conversation.

I let out a huge breath that had been bottled up inside me. My mom looked at me a couple more times. Then she rose from the table, walked over to the counter, and opened a drawer. She pulled the phone book out from the drawer and looked up a number, then grabbed the phone and dialed, her back to me. Art Carter was sipping his coffee while she was on the phone. His back was to me, but then he turned around and looked at me through the window. There was no expression on his face. No hint as to what was going on inside. I started to think that maybe his visit had nothing to do with our conversation the other day, or that maybe he'd come over to complain to my mother about my going to his house again to discuss my plan. What if he was asking my mother to keep me away from him again?

My mother returned to the table, and the conversation between her and Art Carter seemed slower now, friendlier, and less businesslike.

A few minutes later I heard a car engine rattle up to our house with the recognizable sound of an old Volkswagen. I heard car doors closing. Stepping onto the deck were Bliss's parents, with Bliss in tow.

Bliss ran past them to me. "What's going on?" she asked me. Bliss's parents didn't even need to knock on the door; my mom opened the door and invited them in immediately. I continued to watch through the window.

"Answer me, Evie!" Bliss demanded. "My parents got a phone call from your mom asking if they could come over, so they left Buzzy with the neighbor and we drove over here." Bliss shot questions as me faster than I could register them in my brain. "What's going on? Are we in trouble or something? Did your mom find out that we're investigating David's death?"

"No, at least I don't think so," I said slowly while my eyes remained glued to the window. "And if someone is in trouble, it's going to be just me."

"Why, what did you do?" she asked.

I took a deep breath and filled Bliss in. I told her about how the idea had come to me when she'd asked me to listen to the river whisper, and how I'd gone to see Art Carter and then how Art Carter showed up here today, and why I thought her parents were in my house talking with my mom and Art Carter. When I was finished, we both looked in through the window with anticipation, waiting for the outcome. At one point I saw my mom get up and walk over to a tissue box and offer Bliss's mom a tissue. Maggie took it and dabbed at her eyes, which made me worry.

Bliss's parents stood and Bliss's' father, Tom, put his arm around his wife. He reached out and shook my mom's hand and then Art Carter's hand. Both of Bliss's parents looked shocked, but pleased. My mom escorted everyone to the door.

When the door opened, both Bliss and I walked over to the doorway.

"We'll see you at the bank Monday morning to draw up the paperwork," my mother said to Maggie and Tom.

Bliss was asking her parents a million questions as they walked to their car. Art Carter turned to me and with a slight grin he nodded at me, then turned to my mom and said, "I'll have the formal proposal for you by Monday morning for the paperwork." Then he strode across the deck. I watched him climb into his truck and drive off.

My mom and I were left standing on the deck. She looked at me. "It seems you've been quite busy lately. Let's go inside and talk and you can fill me in on some of the gaps that Mr. Carter might have left out."

As I entered the house, the warmth enveloped me immediately. I hadn't realized how cold I had gotten from sitting outside.

My mom put a kettle on the stove. "It seems like a good day for hot chocolate," she said, sitting down across from me at the table. "My, my, my," she said in a drawn-out, exaggerated manner. "It's quite a predicament you've placed me in. Would you like to explain how this all came about?"

"Sure, but Mom, first tell me, is it going to happen?"

"Yes, I think we settled the matter and Bliss's family will get their house back." Then the whole thing flowed out of me. I told her how I knew that Mr. Carter used to have his own contractor's business building houses and raising houses above the flood level, and that Bliss had told me how her family lost their house in a flood because it wasn't raised. "And I figured if Mr. Carter could price the job right that maybe you could help get Bliss's family a loan."

"Mr. Carter's estimate *is* rather generous. ... To be honest I don't know how he's going to make money off this job. He did say that much of the wood in the structural support of the home is still good. The paperwork will be taken care of, and with Mr. Carter raising the house in the process, or rebuilding, Bliss's family will be able to get flood insurance this time, which helps with the loan paperwork. Mr. Carter even seemed to think he could start work this week so he might finish the job before winter."

The kettle whistled and my mom rose from the table and took it off the stove. She poured packets of hot chocolate mix into two mugs and continued to talk to me. "Evie, you are a bright young lady, but writing up this loan is a bit of a risk for the bank. What if I hadn't been able to do it?"

When she said that, I remembered our conversation earlier that morning. "Look, they're probably going to close this branch soon anyway. What's there to lose?"

My mom chuckled. "Funny, I thought the same thing while talking with Mr. Carter."

Although my mood improved somewhat with the hope that Bliss and her family might get their home back, I still felt gloomy about the prospect of moving again. The weather seemed to match my mood right through the weekend.

Chapter 13
Thanks and Goodbye

Monday morning Bliss and I walked to school at a rapid pace, not only because it was a chilly morning, but also because she talked a mile a minute about rebuilding the house. She must have thanked me a hundred times.

Halfway to school she grabbed my backpack and turned me to face her. "Evie, you have no idea what this means to my family." Then she hugged me and we stood in the middle of the creek bed hugging. I wanted to cry. I was happy for her, but I felt rotten too. I finally had a friend I trusted. At that moment as she hugged me, I realized that I had never really trusted my friends back in Oceanside. They gossiped so much … and I had gossiped with them. I had changed so much in the short time I'd known Bliss. She was the first one to believe me about David. How was I going to tell her that I might have to move?

"What's going on?" David popped up, and I pulled away from Bliss.

"David's here." I was glad for the interruption, because if Bliss kept thanking me and hugging me, I was going to scream.

"David," she said, looking around but not quite placing her eyes in the right direction, "your dad is the greatest!"

"What's she talking about?" David asked me.

"Oh no, that's right!" I said to Bliss. "David doesn't know about any of this."

"Know about what?" he asked warily. "What has happened?"

I told David everything about his father's visit over the weekend, and Bliss filled in information as I went along, like it was the most normal thing in the world for the two of us to be talking to a ghost.

When we finished filling David in, he smirked, "Well, that explains it."

"Explains what?" I asked.

"I went to see my father last night and he was actually cleaning the kitchen." I chuckled. After having seen Art Carter's kitchen I understood why that would be such an unusual sight. Then David acted with a bit of humility, which he rarely did, and said, "Thank you, Evie."

Ugh! Now I had two people thanking me. Or one person and one ghost … either way, two friends I might have to move away from. I sighed and we continued walking to school.

Reading buddies was on Mondays, so off we went to the library in our lines.

Lizzy ran up to me as soon as I walked through the library door. She grabbed my hand and pulled me to a cozy corner in the library away from everyone else.

"Are you going to finish the story about Francisco?" she asked eagerly.

"Of course. Now where did I leave off?" I asked, even though I knew exactly where I'd left the story.

"Francisco felt the shark in the water."

"Oh yes, and he was scared that he was about to be eaten. Well, Francisco put his hand out to block the attack of the shark. He felt a large jolt, but instead of sharp teeth, it was the slimy skin on the side of the shark that slammed into him. There was something else in the water attacking the shark. Over and over something was banging into the large sea beast. Poor Francisco, though, he'd been under water so long, he couldn't hold his breath any longer and had begun to swallow water. Everything went black—he was sure that this was the end. However, the next thing Francisco knew, he was coughing and sputtering up water. He was at the surface. As he opened his eyes, the bright light blinded him and he wasn't sure where he was, but he felt the sensation of moving across the top of the water. He was alive!"

Lizzy interjected, "It was the dolphin, wasn't it? Paulina came and saved him." Lizzy had interrupted very little while listening but sat wide-eyed, hanging on every word. I was quite impressed at how well she listened for being just a kindergartner.

"Yes. Paulina attacked the shark from the side, just as the shark was about to take a chomp out of Francisco. The dolphin lifted Francisco to the surface and began carrying him to a nearby island. Once they reached the shallow water, Francisco let go of the dolphin's fin. He stood in the waist-high water and spoke softly to the dolphin. 'Oh Paulina, you saved me like I saved you so many years ago. ... You came back just to help me. I love you.' As he spoke, the dolphin swam circles around him. Then it lifted its nose out of the water and bellowed a chattering sound at Francisco and nodded its head. Then Paulina dove into the water and jumped out to show off a flip in the air, and then she swam away, leaving Francisco weeping with sadness and happiness all mixed in together. He turned and walked to shore."

When I was finished with the story, Lizzy clapped her hands with delight.

"That was great!" she screeched. I smiled at the compliment.

As the rest of the kids were putting books away, Lizzy asked, "Evie, can you help me after school?"

"With what?"

She looked down at the floor and fidgeted with her hands. "My mom is picking me up after school. She never picks me up. The teacher walks us out to the bus and I take the bus home, but today I'm supposed to wait in the parking lot for my mom, but she said she'd be a little late ... and I'm scared to wait by myself." "Sure, I'll wait with you after school." She raised her head and smiled. "Why is your mom picking you up today anyway?"

"We're going to the hospital ..." She paused, then leaned in and in a whisper said, "To see my sister."

I had forgotten that Lizzy had mentioned her sister before. "That's right, you have an older sister, right?" I asked.

"Yes, but I don't get to see her very often. My mom goes all the time. I asked if I could go this time, and she said that I could." Her eyes were welling up with tears. I decided not to pursue it at that moment because I could tell we were going to have to go back to our classes in a matter of minutes. Everyone was heading for the door. I didn't want to leave Lizzy crying. I placed my hand on her shoulder, and she leaned in and hugged me. My second hug that day, and the second time I felt like crying.

I worried about Lizzy all day and completely forgot about solving David's death for a while. Which was okay because everyone seemed preoccupied with other things. Bliss was excited about the house, David seemed delighted about the new change in his father, and Johnny wasn't even at school.

Johnny was absent with a cold. I was sort of glad about Johnny's absence. It had already been an emotionally draining day as I tried to fight back my rotten mood, and seeing Johnny might have completely unglued me when thinking about the possibility of leaving Turnville.

When the end-of-the-day bell rang, I met Bliss to tell her to walk home without me, then hurried to Lizzy's classroom. Lizzy's teacher thanked me for looking out for Lizzy, and I took Lizzy by the hand and we made our way to the parking lot. We stood at the edge of the lot and watched kids walking away in groups while others loaded themselves into cars. Eventually the lineup of parents and cars thinned out until eventually only Lizzy and I were left standing together.

"My mom said she would be just a little late," Lizzy said.

"It's okay, I didn't have anything else to do today. C'mon, let's sit down," and we dropped ourselves onto the curb.

"My sister's at the hospital in Colton," Lizzy said.

"What's wrong with her?"

Before Lizzy could answer me, Ms. Roberts walked by. She stopped when she saw us sitting there. "Do you girls have a ride?" she asked in that concerned teacher tone.

I nodded and Lizzy answered, "Yes, my mom's coming—she's just going to be a little late."

"Okay," said Ms. Roberts. "Have a nice afternoon, but if your mom isn't here within half an hour, you go into the office, okay?"

We assured her that we would. I watched as she walked over to a car three parking spaces away. At the same time I was thinking how difficult it was to believe that Ms. Roberts could have killed David. She was so nice.

As I watched Ms. Roberts fumbling with her keys, I noticed it! The car … it was a different color. It wasn't white, it was deep red. It was a completely different car! Maybe after Bliss and I had asked questions that day, about the car, Ms. Roberts had realized that we were on to her and needed to change cars.

I looked at Lizzy. "Stay here, I'll be right back." I hopped up and trotted over toward Ms. Roberts. "Ms. Roberts," I hollered, trying to get her attention.

"Yes?" She turned toward me as she was unlocking the car.

"Uh … I forgot, do we have a homework assignment in math tonight?" What a dumb thing to ask, but it was the only thing that came to mind. I needed to stall her somehow.

"No, not tonight."

"Oh, okay, thanks." Then trying to sound casual, I said, "Excuse me, Ms. Roberts, but isn't this a different car than the one you had a couple of weeks ago when Bliss and I carried out those boxes?" I knew I was being bold.

"You're observant," she said. I thought she might avoid answering my question, but she continued, "The other car was just a loaner from the garage that was fixing my car. This one's actually mine, and boy, am I glad to have it back." She smiled.

"A loaner?"

"Sure. While the mechanic fixed my car, he loaned me the one you saw last time."

I felt a sense of relief because it meant that Ms. Roberts couldn't have possibly been the one responsible for David's death—she didn't have a white car. Although I felt relieved, I was also frustrated because it meant we no longer had a suspect ... unless ... maybe ... the mechanic? "Ms. Roberts, where is this mechanic?"

"Oh, way out in Lamden Falls. My car broke down when I was visiting my brother there, so I had to take it to someone there. Then of course I needed a car to get back here for work, so the mechanic had one I could use ... for an additional price, of course." She let out a little chuckle of disgust. "Over the weekend I drove to Lamden Falls and picked up my repaired car."

"Oh," I said under my breath, disappointed that the mechanic couldn't be our suspect either because I knew Lamden Falls was more than two hours away.

"Evie, why are you so interested in my car?" She asked it in such a way that made me think that maybe she knew why.

"No reason ... Thanks." I started to walk away.

"Evie, wait." Ms Roberts walked up close to me and in a softer voice said, "Look, I've heard a couple of rumors that maybe you and Bliss are investigating David Carter's death." I was shocked when she said it. Jake was right: people were talking in town. She continued, "Just ... well ... just be careful, okay? Sometimes things aren't what you think they'll be."

I nodded with a dumfounded expression and she grimaced a sort of worried smile and returned to her car.

I walked slowly back to where Lizzy was sitting. I plopped myself back on the curb next to Lizzy as a feeling of aggravation seeped into my body.

"A brain tumor," Lizzy said.

"What's that?" I was confused by her statement.

"That's what's wrong with my sister. … She has a brain tumor." Before I could reply, a car pulled into the parking lot.

"It's my mom," Lizzy said, standing up. I stood with her and took a step back away from the curb so that her mom could bring the car right up to where we were.

I felt lost as all the new information and recent happenings flooded me all at once. We had no suspect. It must difficult for Lizzy to have a sister in the hospital. Did she say brain tumor? I might have to move away and say goodbye to all my friends. One rotten thing on top of another, all jumbled together.

When I looked up, an odd sensation tingled all over my body. Pulling up to the curb was a white car. It reminded me of what my mom had said when she first told me that we were moving to Turnville. She had said that when one door closes, a new door opens. It seemed the minute there was no suspect for David's death, another possibility appeared out of nowhere.

Lizzy's mother rolled down the window on the passenger side. "Come on, Lizzy, get in," she said.

"Mom," Lizzy said as she leaned in toward the window, "this is Evie, my reading buddy."

Her mom seemed worried and nervous. "Hello, Evie. Thanks for waiting with Lizzy. That was very kind of you."

"No problem," I replied.

"Lizzy, get in. We need to get going," she ordered, trying to sound friendly, but it came out strained.

Lizzy opened the back door of the car and said goodbye to me. As I stood and watched them drive off, I began thinking about Lizzy's mom. Why had she been so nervous? Did she somehow know that Bliss and I were asking questions about David? It was evident that people in town were talking. Did she have something to hide? Of course, she might have appeared nervous because she had a daughter in the hospital. That would be reason enough to be worried. Regardless, I did know one thing: we had a new suspect!

Chapter 14
If They Holler, Let 'em Go

Instead of going home through the creek bed, like I normally did, I ran down the road that led to Bliss's trailer park. I wanted to tell Bliss and David what I had discovered: Ms. Roberts was off the hook, but now we had a new suspect. The trailer park had an arch over the entrance saying Garden Mobile Estates. I laughed inwardly as I passed under the arch, because the idea of calling a trailer park "estates" seemed funny. I knocked on the door of Bliss's trailer home, but there was no answer. Disappointed, I stepped away from the trailer to head home, when out of the corner of my eye I saw Bliss sitting at the edge of the creek bed on the makeshift bench.

I walked up to her. "Hey there."

She turned with a jump, and I realized that she had been absorbed in reading a book. She put it down on the bench next to her.

"I was just trying to get my mind off what happened at the bank today. My parents aren't back yet, so I don't know how it went."

Maybe Bliss and I were more alike than I thought. I often turned to a book to get things off my mind. "I'm sure it went okay," I said, trying to sound reassuring.

I leaned in close to her and whispered, "I have some new, interesting developments on David's case."

"What'd you find out?" she asked.

"Ugh. I wish David were here so I wouldn't have to repeat it all again later. Just like him—he shows up when I don't want him to and is nowhere to be found when I actually want him here."

Bliss stood up. "David," she yelled while looking around. She cupped her hands to her mouth. "Yoo hoo, David, where are you?" she yelled louder.

It made me nervous to see her standing there yelling for a ghost that she couldn't even see. I began to look around for anyone who might see us. There was no one around. "Daaaavid," she yelled again. After waiting a moment she turned and looked at me. "Anything yet? Is he here?"

"No," I said laughing.

"What, what's so funny?" she asked.

"Nothing," I said.

"Well, maybe since you're the one who can see him, he can hear your voice and not mine. ... You try."

"Uh ... I don't think so."

"Come on, Evie, why are you always afraid to try new things? Do you really care what other people think?"

Was she right? Was I afraid of trying new stuff? I thought about swimming in the river, going to the police station, and facing Art Carter. ... I felt that I was pretty brave to do all those things. It seemed to me I was trying new things on a weekly basis. However, she was right about me in one way: I did seem to care what others thought of me.

I took a deep breath. "David," I yelled halfheartedly.

"Ah, c'mon, you can do better than that," Bliss taunted.

I glanced around again, and this time I belted it out. "David, where are you when we need you? We have news for you!" I screamed.

Bliss started giggling and I did too. I knew how silly we probably looked, but it felt good.

"DAVID," we yelled together loud enough that there was a slight echo from the creek bed. Then we broke down in complete laughter, doubling over and clutching our stomachs. Once our laughter subsided, I took one last look around. ... Unfortunately there was no David to be seen. I guess it wasn't up to me when he showed up, it was up to him.

So, without David I filled Bliss in on all that I had found out. When I was finished, I could tell she was impressed.

That evening when my mom got home, she told me the good news about Bliss's house and how all the loan paperwork went smoothly and that there was going to be a work party on Saturday, a sort of groundbreaking celebration. She said that since this whole thing was my idea, it was important that I be there. Of course I wouldn't have missed it for the world. However, if I had known then everything that was going to happen that weekend, perhaps I wouldn't have been so eager to go.

Chapter 15
Digging Deeper

For the first time since living in Turnville the rest of the week felt somewhat normal. Johnny had returned to school by Wednesday, but sounded stuffed up … so kissing was definitely out. He started eating lunch with Bliss and me, and the three of us continued to walk home together. After a couple of days Jake tried to give Johnny a bad time about walking home with a couple of "dumb girls," but Johnny gave him a warning glare, and that seemed to settle things enough that Jake left us alone.

The only thing still missing was David. I had wondered about him ever since Bliss and I had tried hollering for him that day. He hadn't popped up in days and I found myself missing him, and even though I didn't miss trying to hide talking to him, he was my friend and I was worried.

Six days went by without having seen David and I wondered if maybe I wasn't able to see him anymore. It wasn't like David to miss school, ghost or not. Perhaps he had disappeared for good and wasn't coming back. That would be awful because I hadn't been able to say goodbye.

Or maybe he *was* there, but for some reason I couldn't see him anymore.

While walking alone in the creek bed Friday morning on my way to pick up Bliss for school, a loud "Boo" broke the silence like a sonic boom. I must have jumped three feet in the air. I turned around and there was David, laughing at the fact that he had scared me.

"Boy, you sure have gotten jumpy," he snickered.

I would have hugged him if I'd thought I could hug a ghost, because I really had missed him. Instead I put on my angry face. "Where have you been?" I demanded. And for the first time I didn't look around to see who might see me talking to the air.

"Ah, that's sweet. Did you miss me?" He giggled some more.

"No! Definitely not. ... Well ... maybe ... a little." I warmed up to him, as his smile was infectious. "Where have you been anyhow? Things haven't been quite the same without you."

"Yeah, I know, I grow on people that way."

Then David told me that he had been watching his dad for the last few days. He told me it was the first time he had seen his dad doing stuff other than working in his wood shop being sad and angry. When I asked him what kinds of things his dad had been doing, David told me that Art Carter had met with some of his old crew members to work on Bliss's house. He'd bought supplies, drafted plans, and taken measurements at the site.

"It was great to see him getting back into work and talking with other people," David said. "I think he's actually excited about this job."

I nodded, then took up walking toward Bliss's again. David jumped in stride next to me and I filled him in on the new developments of his case.

"That's great," he said. "So what's your plan to find out more?"

I realized that we really didn't have a plan. I didn't know how we were going to talk to Lizzy's mom. I didn't even know when or if I was going to see Lizzy's mom again.

"I've got an idea," David said. "Why don't you try questioning Lizzy? She's so young she wouldn't wonder why you were asking questions about her mom or her mom's car."

I knew David was right, but it felt wrong to trick Lizzy like that. She trusted me, she was opening up to me, she liked my Nonno's stories. She was the first little kid that I'd ever related to and that related to me. She didn't make me nervous or jumpy like most little kids. And deep down I knew she was the only one that now shared a piece of my Nonno.

"Yeah, maybe," I said. Bliss joined us and we continued on to school.

When we arrived at school, there was still about ten minutes before the bell would ring, so we looked around for Lizzy. The entire time while searching the play yard I felt miserable inside, and honestly, I wasn't looking very hard. How could I help David without breaking Lizzy's trust?

Five minutes passed and we hadn't found her yet. I started to think that maybe we wouldn't find her and I'd be off the hook ... at least for now. Then I heard Bliss call out over toward the swing set, "Hey ... Hi, Lizzy." Bliss looked back at me and motioned for me to catch up to her. The two of us walked toward the swings. My heart felt heavy. Lizzy was waiting for a swing to be freed up.

"Hi there, Lizzy," Bliss said in her sweet singsongy voice that she often used with her little brother.

I knew Lizzy didn't like strangers much. I gave Bliss a look and she seemed to understand and backed away. I put my arm around Lizzy's shoulder and pulled her away. When we were out of earshot of everyone, I asked, "How's your sister doing?" I was avoiding questions about her mom I just didn't want to ask.

"Not too well. I'm going to the hospital again this weekend to see her. My mom doesn't let me go very often, but lately she's been telling me it's okay if I come."

"I'm … I'm … sorry about your sister" was all I could think to say.

Lizzy grabbed my hand in a familiar manner. "Evie, you remind me a lot of her. She used to tell me wild stories. She has a great imagination, just like you. We always played pretend games, and she could make-believe great places for us to visit with castles and dragons and …" Her voice trailed off. "I really miss her." The bell rang and Lizzy gave me a hug. I watched her trot off to class, leaving me standing there. Bliss came over as soon as Lizzy was gone.

"Well?" Bliss asked.

"There wasn't enough time," I lied. "I'll have to try and talk to her again later."

"That's all right," Bliss said. "Maybe Monday during reading-buddy time you can try again."

"Sure," I replied halfheartedly.

Chapter 16
Work Party

Early Saturday morning my mom knocked on my door. "Get up and at 'em. We're going to the groundbreaking party." Even though I was excited about going, it was still difficult to drag myself out of the comfort of the warm covers.

Pancakes were waiting for me on the table, steam still floating from the tops of them. I gobbled them up and guzzled a glass of orange juice, and then off we went.

The sun was peeking out from behind a few clouds, making it pleasant enough for us to walk. I carried a picnic basket full of sandwiches that my mom had made for everyone, and she carried a large canvas bag full of apples and sodas.

As we approached the house, the place was popping with activity. Bliss was helping her mom carry some old lumber toward a pile that was already getting quite large. Bliss nodded in my direction and yelled out a hello since she couldn't wave while carrying the wood.

"Evie, why don't you put the picnic stuff down over by that large fallen tree, in the shade for later." My mother handed me the canvas bag. She walked over to Art Carter and I could faintly hear her ask what she could do to help out. I walked to the tree and placed the lunch supplies down, then ran over to Bliss and grabbed part of the wood she was carrying and helped carry it.

Everyone seemed to have jobs throughout the morning. Bliss and I helped Maggie carry old lumber and pruning clippings out of the way into a pile to be hauled off later, and when we weren't moving things, we were chasing after Buzzy, trying to keep him out of the way.

Tom, Bliss's dad, was working with a couple of guys who were part of Art Carter's work crew. They were pulling out parts of the house like cabinets and drywall and old doors. They were a three-man demolition crew. It was strange to see a house gutted so quickly.

My mom and Art Carter were on the roof pulling off old shingles and tossing them into a large trash containter that had been set up directly next to the house. My mother looked perfectly capable of keeping up with Art Carter in her jeans and leather gloves. I realized just how independent she was. However, a couple of times I looked up at the roof to see her laughing and throwing her head back to get her hair out of the way. If I hadn't known better, I would have thought that she was flirting. That thought struck me hard. I mean, could she actually be flirting? I looked at Art Carter. He smiled softly at my mom, and a couple of times I thought I caught him trying to catch a glimpse of her when she wasn't looking. Flirting would be one thing, but with HIM? With Mr. Carter?

My mom had been single since I could remember. Not once could I recall her going on a date or showing interest in someone as I was growing up. I always thought I wanted her to go out with someone, but while watching her on the roof with Art Carter, I had mixed feelings about it. One part of me wanted her to be happy, another part of me was jealous, and yet another part was appalled that of all people, it was Art Carter. But then, didn't he deserve some happiness too? But did it need to be with *my* mother?

My mom had always focused her attention on me, and we had a good relationship. Many of my old friends had told me that they envied me because it was so easy to talk with my mom. What if she started dating? Would her seeing someone interfere with our relationship? Could I still talk with her about private things? Would Art Carter try to tell me what to do? I was starting to think that Art Carter was probably a nice enough guy. I looked at all the activity around me and realized all that he had done for Bliss and her family. He had actually listened to my crazy idea, but he was gloomy and angry. I looked up to the roof again and saw Mr. Carter smiling.

I looked around for David. Maybe I could talk to him about this. I saw him sitting on the fallen log near the picnic supplies watching all that was going on. Maggie and Bliss were occupied with Buzzy for the moment, so I walked over to David.

I didn't want anyone to see me talking to David, especially my mom or Art Carter. I took a soda out from the canvas bag and popped it open. I sat down on the log, next to David, and observed the scene in front of me.

Everyone was working together. It sort of felt as if there was a party going on. ... I understood what they meant by a work party. There was a real positive energy to it all. I scanned David's face; he was the only one not smiling. I was surprised. I had thought it would make him happy to see his dad out of the house and Bliss getting her house back.

I put the soda can to my mouth to disguise my talking. I pretended to take a drink. "What's wrong?" I asked from behind the soda can.

David said nothing; he just let out a deep sigh.

"Aren't you happy that your dad is working again?" I asked, pretending to take another sip.

"Yeah, I guess, but Evie, look at me. I can't do anything to help out. I'm sitting here observing life, not participating in it. ... How much fun is that?"

I had never really thought about it, but it wasn't like David could just jump in and start lifting lumber. And nobody talked to him except me.

"Evie," he pleaded earnestly. "You have to find out who killed me ... you just have to. I can't go on like this just observing life and never being part of it. It's awful!" Then he stood up and moved in front of me, bent over, and pushed his face close up to mine. "Talk to Lizzy ... soon!" And before I could say anything else, he disappeared. The look on his face lingered in my mind. As much as I didn't want to hurt Lizzy, I owed this to David. It was the one thing I had promised to do that first day we met.

I really took a drink from my soda when Bliss walked over and I offered her some lunch. I pulled out sandwiches and sodas, and before I knew it, the entire group was lined up on the fallen tree like worn-out soldiers. Bliss and Buzzy were the only two not sitting on the tree. Bliss was sitting on the ground in front of me with her legs crossed and the two of us were talking about all that we had accomplished. Buzzy was running around chasing a squirrel that was approaching us to get some lunch leftovers. There was a low rumble of multiple conversations along the tree. Everyone thanked my mom for making lunch. It felt nice to be part of all the activity, but still David was in my thoughts, and how he wasn't able to be part of this experience.

After lunch people asked Mr. Carter what they could do next for the rest of the afternoon.

"Actually," Mr. Carter said, "we got a great start on things, and clearing the way for equipment and new supplies is what needed to be done today. What I really need to do is go into Colton this afternoon and order lumber and supplies." He looked around and made eye contact with everyone; it was obvious he wasn't comfortable making speeches. "I truly appreciate all the help this morning, but for now everyone can head home. My crew and I will get back to work this week when supplies are delivered."

Tom stood and walked over to Mr. Carter and my mother. "I just want to thank you both for making this possible. We never would have dreamed that this kind of generosity existed in Turnville." Maggie nodded in agreement.

I could see my mom's eyes well up a little, but Mr. Carter said, "It's just a job, like any other job. Besides, you're paying for the work." I could tell Mr. Carter didn't like all the attention. He had made the job affordable, and we all knew it.

Everyone gathered tools that they had brought and packed up to go home. Art Carter and my mother were loading things into the back of his truck. I walked over to them. "Mr. Carter?" I asked. "Are you heading into Colton right now?"

"Yes," he answered.

"Can I go with you?" It wasn't that I really wanted to ride with Art Carter, but I needed to go into Colton.

My mom piped in, "Whatever for?"

"Well, the kindergartner who's my reading buddy is in town today visiting her sister in the hospital, and I'd like to stop by and give her some support." It was mostly the truth.

My mom smiled at the comment. I could tell she was pleased with my supposed thoughtfulness for someone else's well-being. I couldn't look her in the eye, though, because I knew there was another motive behind my visit, one that didn't feel so nice.

Mr. Carter was standoffish about the idea, and to be honest I was a little nervous about the prospect of it too, but my mother looked over at Art Carter with raised eyebrows. "Well, it's okay with me, if you don't mind."

"Uh ... well." I could tell he wanted to say no, but he looked at my mom's face, and not wanting to disappoint her, said, "Sure. ... Hop in" and motioned for me to go around to the passenger side of the truck.

Chapter 17
Truth and Consequences

There was an uncomfortable silence in the truck as we made our way along River Road toward Colton. The blues music softly playing from the CD player seemed like suitable music for Art Carter. I saw a CD case sitting between us with the title *Stand Back! Here Comes Charley Musselwhite's South Side Band* on the cover. An instrumental song came on that seemed incredibly melancholy. I picked up the jewel case and looked at cut 12, the number the CD player was displaying. The title of the song was "Sad Day." It figured! Art Carter reached over and turned the volume up. The music seemed to surround us and fill the space between us at the same time. My heart ached as I listened to it.

I stared out the window, trying to figure out what I was going to say to Lizzy and maybe even her mother. We hit a bump and it jostled me out of my daze. I looked at Art Carter. He kept his eyes on the road and never once looked over at me to talk to me like my mom did when we drove somewhere. I could tell he was uncomfortable having me in the truck, which made me even more uncomfortable than I already felt. I looked at his profile. He had a strong, square jaw and I could tell he hadn't shaved that morning. He had small lines around the sides of his eyes that gave him a little worn look, but they seemed sort of kind in a way. I never would have thought of Art Carter as kind—until he took the job on Bliss's house. I tried to see him from my mom's perspective; had she really been flirting with him? I guess he wasn't that bad looking, and he was about the same age as my mom. I saw Mr. Carter grind his teeth a little and I could tell he sensed that I was looking at him. I turned and looked out the window for the remainder of the drive.

As we drove through Colton, Mr. Carter pointed to a three-story box-shaped building. "That's the hospital there. I'll be parking just a couple of blocks away, so you can walk." I was grateful for the help; I'd never been to Colton before and wouldn't have known my way around.

He pulled the truck into a parking place in front of an old western-style building; it was a hardware and lumber store. We both climbed out of the truck. Mr. Carter walked around the truck to the sidewalk next to me. He spoke sternly. "Be careful in town, and don't go anywhere else except that hospital, you hear? I don't like being responsible for someone else's kid." He walked toward the store, but then turned back to me and said, "Be back at this truck in forty-five minutes, okay?" I nodded.

On my short walk to the hospital I took a good look at Colton. It seemed a nice enough town, clean looking, but it was different from Turnville. Colton had a sanitized feel to it. In Turnville, hills and large redwood groves surrounded the downtown, making it feel nestled in and secure, whereas Colton was flat, plain, and open. Colton was more modern looking, the only trees were those purposely planted at the side of the road, and they seemed scrawny. It made me appreciate Turnville, and I realized just how much I didn't want to leave it.

I arrived at the hospital and realized that I hadn't a clue how to locate Lizzy's sister. I didn't know Lizzy's last name, let alone her sister's first name, so I didn't want to ask at the front desk. I scanned a directory sign and looked for pediatrics, or the children's ward. I figured that that would be where Lizzy's sister was. It was on the third floor, so I made my way to the elevator.

On the third floor, I walked down the corridor, trying to appear like I knew where I was going while discreetly peeking into the hospital rooms to search for Lizzy or her mother. I didn't know what her sister looked like, so it seemed my best option.

Hospitals gave me the creeps; they had that sterile smell of sickness and death mixed in with the odor of urine, and it caused my nose to wrinkle. It reminded me of when Nonno had had his heart attack. I recalled when I had visited him in the hospital. It had been horrible seeing him in the bed with so many tubes hanging out of his mouth and arm. He looked weak and tiny lying there, and he couldn't talk; I didn't know if he even knew I was there. The next day after I had visited him, he died. I tried to block the memory out of my mind as I wandered the hallway.

I had already walked three-fourths of the way down the hallway and hadn't seen either Lizzy or her mother. I was beginning to think that perhaps I wasn't going to find them. However, in the second-to-the-last room near the end of the hallway, I peeked in and there was Lizzy's mother, sitting in a chair reading aloud from a book to a girl in a hospital bed.

The girl reminded me so much of my Nonno, it bothered me. She didn't appear to be conscious. She was bald, thin, pale, and, just like Nonno, had tubes connected to her. The tubes seemed attached everywhere: in her arm, her leg, her mouth, her nose.

At first Lizzy's mom didn't see me. I was surprised that Lizzy wasn't there because she had told me that she would be there today.

As I entered the room, Lizzy's mom must have caught my movement from the corner of her eye. She looked up. She placed the book in her lap and took in a deep breath.

"Hello," I said, sounding braver than I actually felt. Inside I was shaking.

"Hi," she answered.

"I'm sorry to interrupt. … It's just that Lizzy said she was going to be here today … and … well, I thought …" My voice trailed off, not sure how to finish my sentence.

"She's here. She's down the hall in the cafeteria getting a candy bar."

I sensed that Lizzy's mom was upset, but she stayed calm.

"Is this your other daughter?" I asked.

"Yes, this is my daughter Tabitha."

"Can she hear us?"

"I'd like to think she can. I read to her often." She paused. "You know, Evie, she'd be in the eighth grade like you. Lizzy tells me a lot about you. She says that you remind her of Tabby." She appeared lost in thought as she went on. "She never got to attend regular school like Lizzy; I always had to home-school her. She was diagnosed with the brain tumor when she was five. We took her to all sorts of specialists, and she underwent torturous treatments—radiation, chemotherapy—and then things seemed to get better. The tumor went into remission for a few years. ... She was starting to look forward to attending regular school ... until ..." Her reminiscing was cut off by another figure entering the room. I looked up, and there was Art Carter.

"Excuse me," he apologized to Lizzy's mom. Then he looked at me. "I finished up early, and I just ... uh ... got a little ... worried ... and I thought I'd see if I could find you."

"It hasn't been forty-five minutes yet," I said.

He seemed embarrassed. "No, not yet, but I ..." His voice trailed off as his gaze shifted to where Tabitha lay in the hospital bed. I could tell he was thinking about David, and the thought occurred to me that maybe he'd gotten worried about me because of what had happened to David. That explained why he'd said that he didn't like being responsible for other people's kids.

What happened next surprised me the most. We were interrupted by a sobbing that came from Lizzy's mom. Her sobbing grew louder, to an almost uncontrollable level. Neither Mr. Carter nor I knew what to do. I assumed she was crying because of Tabitha, but then she grabbed a tissue from the box next to her, took a deep breath to get herself under control, and began speaking ... to Mr. Carter.

"Mr. Carter," she said, fidgeting with the tissue in her hands. "I owe you a deep and immense apology." I looked over at Art Carter, who seemed confused.

"No," he answered. "I apologize for interrupting."

In very slow, deliberate words, Lizzy's mom said, "I'm the one responsible."

I had a suspicion of what she meant, but it was obvious that Art Carter hadn't a clue.

She continued, "I'm the one who hit David that terrible day in front of the school." I looked over at Art Carter. I watched his face as the words slowly sank in. His face turned bright red, and I could see his nostrils flare. He seemed to be restraining himself, and said nothing; he just stared at Lizzy's mom with a look of disbelief.

When Mr. Carter remained silent, Lizzy's mom continued, "I'm so, so sorry. I'm so terribly sorry. That was the day that Tabitha"—she nodded toward her daughter—"fell and became unconscious. … It was the day we discovered that she'd come out of remission, and that the brain tumor had taken over." I could see Art Carter's eyes dart over to Tabitha, but his expression remained hard and unmoving. "She's never recovered since that day."

Lizzy's mom dabbed at her eyes. "Mr. Carter, I'm losing a child, and I understand what it's like to lose a child: I've been losing my daughter ever since that day, watching her slip further away from me." I heard Art Carter snort. "I know I can never replace your loss. … I can only offer that I *will* turn myself in."

She stood and took a step toward Art Carter, who backed away a step. "Mr. Carter, my daughter doesn't have much time. … Just let me say goodbye. … The doctors say it could be any day now. When she goes, I'll turn myself in. I'll tell them everything. I know I'm asking a lot, but wouldn't you, if you could, say goodbye to David? Please. I'm begging you … please."

I couldn't take my eyes off Art Carter. I couldn't move. The very air I tried to breathe was frozen, creating a tightness in my chest. His nostrils flared one more time. Without speaking he nodded curtly to Lizzy's mom, then quickly turned and briskly walked out of the room. My eyes focused on Lizzy's mom. She fell to her knees on the floor, dropped her head between her hands, and began sobbing again.

"Evie! You're here!" I turned around to see Lizzy run into the room. She threw her arms around my waist and hugged me tightly. "Look, Mama, Evie came to meet Tabitha!"

Lizzy's mom raised her head and looked me straight in the eyes. "I hope you're happy," she said.

I was anything but happy. I had never felt so miserable in all my life. I wanted out of that hospital room more than anything in the world, and if I had let my initial instincts take over, I would have been halfway down the hallway, running at top speed. But then I felt Lizzy's little hand in mine, and I knew I couldn't leave at that very moment.

"Gosh, Lizzy, that candy bar you have there sure looks good," I said. "Can you show me where you got it? I think I'd like one too." I avoided her mother's hard gaze.

"Sure," Lizzy said. She looked at her mother kneeling on the floor, and although I could tell she didn't understand what had taken place just moments before her arrival, she did seem to sense that she should leave her mom alone, so she turned and led me away to the cafeteria.

After spending a little time with Lizzy, I walked back to Art Carter's truck, not even sure if he would still be there waiting for me. As I approached it, I could see him leaning against the truck staring off in my direction.

When he saw me walking toward him, he climbed inside. I silently crawled into the cab next to him.

On the way home it was completely silent—there wasn't even any music on this time. I glanced up at Art Carter from time to time and could see his face contorted with anger and pain. He looked much like he had that first day I had knocked at his door.

We entered downtown Turnville, and I couldn't hold back anymore. "Mr. Carter … you can't turn her in," I said.

"And why not?" he asked, keeping his eyes forward.

"Because David wouldn't want you to," I replied.

Art Carter turned his head and I could see the fire in his eyes. I was actually a little worried that we were going to crash. It was as if he didn't even care about the road in front of him. "What are you saying? Is David here right now in this truck telling you this? Is he telling you he doesn't want the woman who killed him to go to jail for her crime?"

"No," I said, looking down. "But I know David … and I know that he wouldn't want Lizzy to lose her sister and then lose her mother. …" Before I could finish, he cut me off.

"You do NOT know David!" he yelled. "He died before you ever moved here!"

He looked back at the road, breathing heavily, almost panting. How was I ever going to explain? There was no way I was going to be able to make him understand.

"Then don't do it because of David. … Instead don't turn her in because it's the right thing to do," I said, trying to stay calm but feeling angry myself. He didn't respond so I asked, "What about doing the right thing?"

We pulled up in front of my house. Mr. Carter stopped the truck but left the motor running, and then he answered my question with one of his own. "What about justice? She took away my son."

I climbed down from the cab out of the truck, and stood there with the door open and faced him. "It seems to me that God has already served his own justice. … You lost a child and so will she, but what did Lizzy do to deserve this justice of yours?" I slammed the truck door before he could reply.

I watched him back up his truck and drive away, leaving me standing there alone. I stared at my house. I didn't want to go in. I didn't want to face my mother. What would I tell her? That I'd discovered who killed Art Carter's son? I ran down Cherry Lane in the opposite direction of Art Carter's truck all the way to Johnny's house. I knocked on the door and was grateful when Johnny answered the door instead of Jake or one of his parents.

"Evie?" He sounded surprised. He stepped across the threshold and closed the door behind him. I don't know what came over me at that moment, but I threw my arms around his neck and began crying. It was real, uncontrollable bawling. He slipped his arm around my back and let me cry without saying a word. We stood like that a long time. He let me cry into his lower neck and held me without saying a word until slowly my tears subsided.

Johnny pulled back but kept one hand on my arm. He lifted his other hand and wiped the tears off my cheek. It was such a gentle thing to do. Without asking any questions, he took my hand and led me over to a small bench on his front porch.

When my breathing became more even, he spoke. "Now, tell me, what's happened?" And without stopping I told him everything, and without judging me or interrupting he listened.

Chapter 18
Misery Loves Company

I spent the rest of the weekend keeping to myself. Johnny called me a couple of times to make sure I was okay. He asked if I planned on telling Bliss and David. And although I knew I had to, I just wasn't ready yet. So when Monday morning came around, I pretended to be sick and my mom let me stay home. I was glad too because Mondays were also reading-buddy days and I knew I couldn't face Lizzy, knowing what was going to happen once Tabitha died.

About three-thirty that afternoon there was a knock on my door. My mom wasn't home and wouldn't be until at least five or six, so I peeked out the window and saw Bliss standing at my door with David right behind her. I didn't think Bliss knew David was there, but they looked as if they were standing there together. They had come right after school. I answered the door.

"Where were you today?" Bliss asked.

I was wearing my grungy old sweat pants and my soft T-shirt with holes. I took a step outside onto the front deck; I didn't want to risk David seeing the boat. I had almost smashed that boat up when I'd first gotten home from Colton on Saturday because I had been so angry with Mr. Carter. But the boat was also a connection to David, and I just couldn't bring myself to do it.

"Well, where were you?" Bliss repeated.

I lied and told them I didn't feel well. David looked at me suspiciously; I had the distinct feeling that he especially didn't believe me.

"Well, nothing too exciting happened. Besides, you wouldn't have been able to talk with Lizzy about her mom's car during reading buddies today anyway." When Bliss said that, I knew Johnny hadn't told her what had happened. That only endeared me to him more. It meant he respected me and cared enough about me to let me be the one to tell her and David.

Bliss sat down in one of the chairs on the deck. "Lizzy wasn't at school today either." Bliss sighed. The moment Bliss said it, I knew. I knew that Tabitha had died.

Her mom had said that it would be anytime, and after seeing Tabitha in the hospital, even I could tell it would be soon. I just didn't think it would be that soon; I thought it would be at least a couple of days. I felt a crushing sensation on my heart. I couldn't breathe. I felt lightheaded and dizzy.

"Wow, you really don't look too good," Bliss said. I began to lose my balance. Bliss reached out to steady me and took me over to one of the chaise longues. Once I was sitting down, I put my head between my hands and began to cry. Bliss sat on one side of me and David on the other. Once I regained some composure, I told them everything that had happened over the weekend.

When I was finished, we all sat there feeling miserable together.

"All this time I thought it would be a good thing when we discovered who killed David." Bliss sighed.

"And Evie, you were right," David said, "about what you told my dad. I don't want him to turn in Lizzy's mom."

There seemed nothing to say, so we sat in silence for a long time.

David then sat bolt upright. "Hey, why am I still here?"

Now *that* was a good question. Why was David still here? We had all been convinced that if we discovered who had killed him, he could leave and move on to wherever people go when they die—yet here he was, still sitting next to me. Why didn't he move on, especially now that the truth about his death had been uncovered?

Chapter 19
Dinner with Mom

Although having Bliss and David's company had been comforting, I was glad when they finally left. Once they were gone, I returned to moping around the house, which gave me some time to think about things on my own. Now that Tabitha was dead, was Lizzy's mom going to turn herself in? Perhaps Art Carter was going to do it for her? I started to hate him for that. What about Lizzy? Who was going to be there for her?

Around five o'clock the phone rang. It was my mother. She said she would be late because she was going out to dinner with a friend. She wanted to make sure that I would be okay and was checking in to see how I was feeling. I was relieved that she was going to be late; it would have been hard to hide my feelings from her. Maybe if I was lucky I could already be in bed by the time she got home.

When I heard her car drive up around seven, I was on the couch curled up in a quilt in front of the TV, not really watching what was on. I heard her come in and place her briefcase and keys on the kitchen table. I expected her to go off to her room and get changed into sweats or something comfortable like she always did when she first got home, but instead she walked into the family room, sat down on the couch by my feet, and placed her hand on my knee. "Do you want to talk about it?" she asked.

"About what?" I asked, playing dumb.

"Honey, I went out to dinner with Art Carter. He told me what happened in Colton."

I couldn't believe it: this so-called "friend" she'd gone out with was Art Carter? I sat up a little bit and stiffened.

"What did he say?" I asked.

My mom was able to relay most of what had happened, even a good deal of the conversation that had taken place between Art Carter and me. I was really surprised at how candid he had been with my mom.

"Evie, Lizzy's sister died last night."

I nodded. I had been right. I had hoped I was wrong.

"So, what's going to happen?" I asked.

"Well, Art has made arrangements with Lizzy's mom. The funeral is Friday. Then on Saturday Art will meet her at the police station. She's agreed to confess everything."

"That's not fair!" I exclaimed. "What about Lizzy? Why does she have to lose both her sister and her mother, both within a week of each other?" "I know this is hard to understand, but I don't know what I'd do if something happened to you like what happened to David."

"You wouldn't turn in Lizzy's mom. ... I know you wouldn't, because you'd know that I wouldn't want you to," I said defiantly. "You're a better person than Mr. Carter!"

"Honey, try to understand, everyone deals with their grief differently. Art lost a son. The woman responsible should be held accountable."

I had nothing more to say. I couldn't believe that my mother was on Art Carter's side. I stood up and stormed off toward my room. Just as I reached the doorway, I turned to my mom and said, "I hope he's worth it, Mom. ... I wonder if having *him* in your life is worth losing me!" I knew they were cruel words, threatening words, but at that moment I would have done anything to ensure that Art Carter wasn't going to be part of our lives. How could someone so heartless and so cold be part of our lives? I wasn't about to let it happen!

Chapter 20
Two Sides of a River

The remainder of the week seemed to pass by in a dreamy sort of surreal haze. I felt like I was going through the motions of life, but wasn't really part of it. … Wasn't that what David said he felt like?

Saturday morning I woke up feeling as if I were a convict waking up to my last meal. I was depressed, and I didn't even want to imagine what the day would be like for Lizzy and her mom. I ate a bowl of oatmeal, then left the house. I walked down Cherry Lane instead of the creek bed that morning and headed for downtown.

I situated myself on one of the benches in town, the one directly across the street from the police station. This had been the bench where Bliss, David, and I had first read the police report.

I wasn't sure how everything was going to happen. I pictured Mr. Carter going inside the building and finding a police officer. Then I imagined the two of them climbing into a patrol car and rushing over to Lizzy's house. I could see them in my mind arresting Lizzy's mom right in front of Lizzy, and Lizzy yelling and crying for her mom to stay.

I tried hard to shut my mind down. ... I didn't like the images that kept coming to the surface.

Art Carter did walk up to the police station, but he didn't go inside. He stood at the base of the steps. He leaned against the hand railing, waiting. He didn't see me at first, but then as he looked around, I could tell he saw me sitting on the bench. His face tightened up a bit, but I kept eye contact with him. I was angry and I wanted him to know it. He was the first to look away. Ha! I thought to myself. He looked down the street in the opposite direction from where he had come. He seemed to see something; he stood up, moving off the railing. I followed his gaze and saw Lizzy's mom walking on the sidewalk toward the police station.

When she arrived, they shook hands and Lizzy's mom began to walk up the stairs, but then Art Carter did something that I didn't expect. He put his hand on her elbow, led her down the steps to the sidewalk, and motioned for her to walk down the sidewalk with him. Lizzy's mom had a hollow, empty look to her face. As they walked together, Art Carter glanced over at me.

Two doors down from the police station was a café. Art Carter opened the door for Lizzy's mom. I watched them sit at a table in the window. At first it didn't seem like much was being said. Coffee was brought over to them. After the waitress walked away, I could see Mr. Carter begin talking. Lizzy's mom lowered her head, and I could see her body shaking. Mr. Carter pulled a napkin from the metal holder on the table and offered it to her. She wiped at her face and blew her nose.

Every now and then I could see Art Carter glance out the window at me.

I felt as if I were watching a silent movie, and although I couldn't hear the words, I tried to imagine what Mr. Carter might be saying at that moment. I was hoping with every fiber of my being that perhaps he was telling her how they both had suffered a loss, how there was a little girl back at her house who needed her now, how going to jail wasn't going to bring David back, how forgiveness was best, not punishment.

There was a part of me that knew I could be wrong. For all I knew, Mr. Carter was just buying her a final coffee before turning her in, asking her for more details about the day David died.

I will never know exactly what was said inside that coffee shop that day, but what happened next is a picture that will be forever seared in my mind. After Art Carter and Lizzy's mom finished their coffee, Art Carter threw some money on the table and the two of them stepped out of the restaurant. In front of the building they shook hands. I could faintly hear Lizzy's mom say, "Thank you, Mr. Carter. You are a kind man." Then she turned away from Art Carter and walked back down the sidewalk in the direction she had first come … past the police station.

Art Carter turned his entire body squarely at me and looked at me from across the street. My mouth was agape and we continued to stare at each other. He nodded ever so slightly, then turned and walked the other direction down the sidewalk. I could see both figures, Mr. Carter and Lizzy's mom, getting farther and farther from each other. Was it true? Nobody was going to go into the police station?

Chapter 21
Found a Home

Things were looking up. Lizzy returned to school a week later. She was still down about her sister, but I was happy to know that she and her mom were together. I know that Lizzy wasn't even aware of what had happened between her mom and Art Carter.

During reading buddies Lizzy said to me, "Maybe Tabitha will be like Paulina was for Francisco, and she'll come back to help me in some way."

I smiled and answered, "You know what? I think she's already watching out for you."

The same day Lizzy returned to school, my mom came home with good news. I was sitting at the kitchen table finishing up my math homework when she arrived home. She walked through the door and went through her regular routine—changed into sweats, took off her makeup, then started making dinner.

Standing at the stove while pouring spaghetti noodles into a large pot she asked, "How was your day?"

"Pretty good," I said. "Lizzy came back to school today."

"Oh, that's good." By the way she spoke, I could tell she had something to tell me but was trying to bait me on and get me to ask.

I grabbed her fish hook and put my pencil down. She raised her eyebrows with a mischievous look. "Okay, Mom," I asked. "How was YOUR day?"

She quickly stepped over to the table and sat down next to me. "I'm so glad you asked. It was amazing!" She appeared to be remembering some extraordinary experience.

"What happened?"

"It was unbelievable. People came to the bank by the dozens today."

"What do you mean?"

"I mean … families came in opening accounts, everything from a hundred dollars to transferring life savings. People applied for loans, wanted to refinance mortgages, some just to say hello and make a deposit. There was actually a line." She paused and smiled in awe. "They kept shaking my hand and commenting on what a good thing the bank had done for Bliss's family.

"People introduced themselves to me, they introduced their grandparents to me, their children to me. … It was as if an old dusty curtain had been lifted and I'd somehow been accepted into this community, that we had been accepted … you and me!" She reached over and placed her hand on top of mine. "You know, it's all because of you, Evie, you and your crazy idea of rebuilding that house. People are embracing us and the bank."

"Does this mean we aren't going to have to move?" I asked.

"I don't think so," she answered. "This is the most business that this branch has ever had, ... It was amazing. ... At one point I was close to tears—it was overwhelming." Her eyes welled up just talking about it.

As she told me about the day, a part of me wondered if the community response was only because of Bliss's house. Did people know about Lizzy's mom too? I don't know if I'll ever be sure. I thought back to some of the warnings we had received throughout the investigation: from Ernie at the police station, from Ms. Roberts. To this day I wonder how much people in town really knew about the hit-and-run.

We celebrated that evening; I had sparkling cider while my mom sipped on a glass of champagne. It was such a relief to know we had finally found a home.

Chapter 22
Open House

The following weeks seemed to sail by. School was going well; I was getting the best grades I think I had ever gotten. I had always been an average student, and now I was almost getting straight As.

I continued to share more of my Nonno's stories with Lizzy every week, and slowly she became more of her old self. I always tried to imagine what it must have felt like for her to lose her sister. One day, while telling her the story about Francisco and the mermaid, Lizzy leaned over and kissed me on the cheek.

"What's that for?" I asked

"For being so much like Tabitha!"

Her comment filled my heart, like an old dried-out sponge that finally gets dunked into a bucket of water.

The whole gang—Bliss, Johnny, David, and I—resumed our walks home together. There were still no kisses from Johnny.

The curious part was why David was still with us. Perhaps he wasn't supposed to leave. I was glad, because I really enjoyed his sense of humor. Bliss and Johnny accepted that he was there and that he was real. I acted as a translator for David in conversations, but he never seemed really happy. I kept thinking about what he had said that day about being an observer and not a participant in life.

My mom began dating Art Carter, but I didn't see much of him because they always went out somewhere else—restaurants, movies, that sort of thing. I was pleased to see my mom happy, but I still wasn't sure how I felt about her finding that happiness with Art Carter. Deep down I knew he was a good man, especially after that day I had seen him outside the coffee shop. I certainly respected him for doing what he did. I wondered if the reason my mom never had him over for dinner was because of my ability to see David, which would upset him, or because of what I had said to my mother about not wanting him to be part of our lives. Either way, until I sorted out my feelings about my mom dating him, it probably was best that I didn't see too much of him.

Autumn crept up fast. The town was preparing for the Annual Harvest Fall Fest. The day of the town parade was also the day of the unveiling of Bliss's house. Everyone was supposed to meet at River Road at the edge of the dirt road that led to the house. It was the first day that I really had the chance to observe my mom and Art Carter together.

Mr. Carter picked up my mother and me in his truck. It all felt incredibly awkward. My mom leaned in to kiss Art, but he was hesitant and glanced over at me. I looked away. What I found most difficult was that David was there too, and I couldn't say anything about it. Did David feel as awkward as I did watching our parents together?

We were the first to arrive at the lane. Shortly afterward, Bliss and her family drove up in their Volkswagen. I could see Johnny approaching on foot and was surprised to see Jake with him. I was impressed that Jake refrained from any jokes or comments. I wondered if Johnny had threatened him.

Other people from town showed up too. Officer Ernie smiled that big, round plum-cheeked smile; he still made me a bit nervous after our meeting at the police station. Others came whom I recognized from around town but didn't know very well. All sorts of people shook hands with Tom and Maggie or Art Carter and my mom. I was surprised how many people my mother knew. She seemed to know their names when she shook hands with them. I realized that she socialized with people around town quite a bit at the bank. All in all there were close to forty people there.

Everyone gathered and walked together down the lane toward the house as if we were part of a big demonstration. Mr. Carter seemed nervous. I saw my mom reach over and take his hand to reassure him, and he smiled weakly.

When the house came into view, I was awestruck. The sight took my breath away; I had never seen such a beautiful home. It looked nothing like it first had when Bliss had brought me there.

The house had been raised up. It was painted a warm, chestnut brown, and skylights had been put in. The thing that impressed me the most was that despite all the newness, the porch swing that Bliss and I had first sat on was still there. But instead of being on the deck where it first was, the swing was hanging from its own specially made structure right in the middle of a spectacular herb garden—an herb garden that had one very large lavender plant in the center. Art Carter had taken such care to preserve the very heart of the property … it was amazing. My eyes welled up. Bliss ran over and gently touched the porch swing, which was stained and carved with intricate designs. Maggie walked up behind her and put her arm around Bliss's shoulder.

I saw Mr. Carter beaming with pride as he watched the scene with my mom next to him. It struck me that he wasn't just a contractor but also an artist.

I was eager to see the inside of the house. Bliss snatched my hand and pulled me along. We climbed a set of stairs; the house had been raised, so that the entire thing was on a second-story level. At the top of the stairs was a wooden arch with carvings. After we passed under the arch, it opened up to a roomy deck. There was a picnic table and a set of Adirondack chairs. The front door was open as others were going in or exiting after touring the house. I could hear people oohing and aahing or complimenting the work Mr. Carter had done. As Bliss and I pushed past a group hovering by the front door, we stood in the center of the living room. Light was streaming down through the new skylights. The place had an airy yet homey feel to it. There was no wall separating the kitchen from the living room, just an island where I could picture a set of bar stools being. There wasn't any furniture in the house yet; the only furniture was the pieces on the deck.

"I can't wait to see my room!" Bliss exclaimed.

I followed her down a hallway into a bedroom. Someone had taken the time to paint a design along the top part of Bliss's wall. They were different flowers, with their names painted in cursive under each flower. It seemed so like Bliss. Bliss turned around and threw her arms around me. "Evie, thank you. ... This is all because of you."

After everyone toured the new house, our mob headed downtown for the Fall Fest parade. Bliss walked with her family, and I could overhear them talking about when they would be moving in. I suddenly felt a presence to my right, and turned to find Johnny walking in stride with me.

"That was a pretty awesome house," he said, and I couldn't have agreed more.

The parade was the hokiest thing I'd ever seen; at times it was hard not to break out in laughter. Tractors rolled down the street with trailers, and trucks had been turned into makeshift floats that were supposed to look like turkeys and teepees. There were people dressed as pilgrims and Indians riding atop them, waving as they made their way down Main Street. One float was a huge pumpkin with about twelve little heads popping out of the top, making it seem as if it were a gigantic egg with little hatchlings inside.

After the parade almost all the townspeople headed to the river park at the end of town. There, a big group of men were standing around large barbecue pits, cooking up turkey legs and other various turkey parts. A large, flat grassy area ended abruptly into a sandy beach that rolled right to the river's edge. There were kids throwing Frisbees and footballs. Families laid out blankets on the grass or tablecloths over picnic tables. Some smaller children were trying to skip rocks into the water. It was like one of those small-town scenes you see in movies, but it was real and I felt comforted by it.

I glanced across the lawn and saw Lizzy with her mother sitting on a blanket away from the crowd a little.

Her mom was braiding Lizzy's hair while Lizzy twisted a piece of grass in her hands.

Bliss was on the other side of the field chasing after Buzzy. I felt someone grab my hand from behind. Startled, I spun around to see Johnny again.

Johnny leaned in close to my right ear and whispered, "C'mon." He walked away, pulling me by the hand. I followed. Quietly we sneaked away from the crowd along the river's edge. I looked back over my shoulder. I didn't want to be seen sneaking away with Johnny Piper. If there was anything I had learned ... this town could talk! There was one person who saw, one person who didn't seem happy in the midst of all this cheer. The look on David's face as Johnny and I tiptoed away haunted me, but I didn't want to turn back.

Johnny and I made our way down a small trail that followed the river's edge. I was curious about where Johnny was taking me, but I still pictured David sitting on the upside-down canoe, watching me take off with Johnny. I knew what was going through David's mind when our eyes met. Once again here he was watching life, not participating in it. As much as I had thought everything was going well for David, I could tell he wanted something more.

Johnny and I came upon a small clearing in the trail. It was different here along the river; it wasn't a sandy beach anymore. The grass was long but had been trampled down flat by others who had walked the trail. The edge of the water wasn't a gradual slope anymore, but instead a muddy marsh that dropped off into a vast deepness of the river. There was a fallen log that made a perfect bench. Johnny pulled me to the log and we sat down.

I felt so conflicted. Part of me was caught up in the excitement of being alone with Johnny. The other part of me held the image of David sitting there watching us walk away.

Johnny guided me to where my heart really wanted to be, the here and now. "Evie," he said, "is … uh … well, is David here right now?"

I smiled. "No. … Well, actually yes." I felt confused. "He is here, in a way, What I mean to say is that he's not actually here with us, but he saw you and I walk away, so he's sort of in my thoughts right now."

Johnny nodded, then looked out across the water. "You know," he said, "when I was in third grade my teacher told us a local Indian tale about how a river whispers." I chuckled, thinking about when Bliss told me that the river whispers.

Even though I knew the answer I asked, "What does it whisper?"

"It whispers to the ocean to tell it that fresh water is on the way." He looked out at the water while placing his hand around my waist. I felt a thrill rush through my bloodstream. "The Indians would set up two camps every year, one at the river and one at the ocean, so they always felt that one talks to the other. Sister River would carry her children out to Mother Ocean."

"Does the river ever whisper to you?" I asked, thinking about when I had heard it speak to me that day with Bliss.

Johnny looked a little embarrassed. "Yeah, sometimes it does."

"What do *you* hear?" I prodded.

"Different things. As a matter of fact when I need answers to a problem, it seems to whisper them." He moved his head away from the river and looked at me. His eyes grabbed mine, not allowing me to look away. We sat there locked in a gaze, but he continued, "As a matter of fact, sometimes I hear it whisper your name softly over and over." And then he leaned in, and finally that kiss that I had been waiting for came, and it was better than my wildest imagination. His lips were soft as they touched mine. Gently he moved his hand from my waist to the back of my head, keeping me locked. At first my eyes were open looking at his cheek, but then they closed and I let my senses take over. So many things to feel: his hand on the back of my head, his soft lips, his smell, the warmth of his body so close to mine. When the kiss was over, he moved away from me slowly and I could feel him looking at me, so I opened my eyes. He was smiling. I smiled back. He reached over and took my hand in both of his and we looked back out at the moving water, neither of us saying anything. We both listened to the river whisper.

"Do you hear anything?" he asked, gesturing toward the water.

"Not yet, but it's a little hard to hear over my heart right now." We both smiled.

I looked across the water again the same way I had that day with Bliss. Gazing over the top of the water, I tried to clear my mind and listen for something. I wasn't sure what, but I knew that I'd hear something. And then it came. … It happened again. I heard the whisper.

I jumped up quickly, startling Johnny because I felt his hand move in a quick motion. He looked at me surprised.

"I have to go," I said. "I know what to do. I know what to do!" I leaned over and kissed Johnny again, quickly this time on the lips. "I'll see you later." I squeezed his hand. Then I jogged down the trail back to the picnic area. I stopped at the canoe where David was still sitting and told him where to meet me later that day. He agreed to be there.

The picnic went by quickly. Afterward Art Carter drove my mom and me home. When we got there, I turned to him and invited him in. He and my mom exchanged a glance. I could tell they were surprised by the invitation, but my mom shrugged and he came in. I suggested my mom's favorite movie and we settled down in the family room to watch it. My mom popped some popcorn, and a cozy feeling overtook the house. I liked it very much, even with Mr. Carter there.

My mom and Art Carter were sitting on the couch together while I sat in the rocking chair that Art had made. Art was in the corner of the couch with my mom leaning into him, his arm casually around her shoulder.

I wasn't paying much attention to the movie, because I was trying to figure out how to do what I had intended to do, what the river had whispered for me to do. I got up and excused myself for a moment. I went to my room, picked up what I had gone in there for, and returned to the family room.

Both my mom and Art Carter felt my presence behind them as I stood there. They both turned to look at me, and Art Carter seemed to understand. My mom leaned forward to allow him to stand up.

Art leaned over and kissed my mom on the forehead. "There's something Evie and I need to do." My mom nodded in reply.

"We'll be back in just a bit," he said. Then, with Art Carter at my side and the boat cradled in my arms, the two of us walked out of the house and down Cherry Lane toward the river.

Chapter 23
Letting Go

As early evening approached, the fog drifted in. I could see it as it slithered between the treetops. The fog surrounded us, creating a silence that could only be revered and embraced. It wasn't a thick fog; it thinly dispersed itself as if it were naturally a part of everything.

As we walked in the foggy silence, I looked down at the boat in my hands. It was still as beautiful and remarkable as the day when I had first laid my eyes on it. It was truly a piece of perfection. I wasn't sure how I was going to let it go. I had gotten used to seeing it first thing every morning when I woke up, sitting on my dresser greeting me.

We reached the end of the lane and entered the trail that wandered down to the river. At first the shrubs and greenery engulfed us, but as we got closer to the water, the trees opened up and the beach awaited us. Standing on the beach was David, waiting right where I had told him to be. When he saw the boat in my arms, he seemed to understand and flashed me that warm smile of his.

I didn't tell Art Carter that David was there; there seemed to be no need. The three of us walked up to the water's edge lined up like a row of birds. I was in the center with Mr. Carter to my left and David to my right.

At the edge of the water Art Carter turned to me and asked, "Are you ready, Evie?" I looked at the boat in my arms, and then I looked at David. David nodded.

"Yes," I said. "Are you?" I asked Art Carter.

Mr. Carter let out a deep breath, as if he had been holding it in for a very long time. "Yes, I think I *am* ready."

I placed half of the boat into Mr. Carter's hands. He gently touched its sides in a loving way. Then with him supporting the bow and me supporting the stern, we placed the boat gently on top of the water. He pushed the bow out first, so that the boat would face downstream, while I kept hold of the back. Once the boat was facing forward, I did what felt like the most difficult thing that I had ever done. ... I let go.

At first the boat moved slowly away from us toward the middle of the river. I looked at David; he had a huge grin on his face. I looked at Art Carter and could see tears welling up in his eyes. I watched the boat again. The fog wrapped its thin fingers around it. The boat began to pick up speed as it found its way into the current.

As I watched it float away, I realized everything I was letting go of. I felt a tug at my heart and heard a final whisper across the water. It said goodbye.

As I watched the boat move farther and farther away from us, I felt that I was finally letting go of my Nonno, of David, of my old life, of all the resentment I harbored. My anger drained out of me, but there wasn't the emptiness that I had expected. Instead I felt other areas of my heart filling up. They filled up with Bliss, with Turnville, with Johnny, even with Art Carter.

The boat was getting fainter and fainter in the fog as it made its way downriver, until finally the fog engulfed it completely. I looked at David. He still had that warm grin on his face, but he was getting fainter too. Like the boat, David was becoming more difficult to see. He was disappearing right before my eyes. As David became fainter, there seemed to be another person, or image, on David's other side taking hold of his hand. It was fainter than David … hardly noticeable. It was my Nonno. Had he been with us all the time? Had I been David's way to reach Mr. Carter, and had David been my Nonno's way to reach me? My Nonno's story came to mind. *Oh Nonno,* I thought, *did you come back just to save me?*

I looked at Art Carter. This time a tear was rolling down his cheek, and then I realized that I was crying too. I turned to look at David and Nonno again, but they were both gone. The last image I had of David was that smile of pure joy on his face. I reached over and slipped my hand into Art Carter's large, rough, sandpaper hand. He let go of my hand and instead put his entire arm around my shoulder and pulled me close to him. We stood like that for a long time looking out into the fog.

When I think about the boat, I'd like to think that it made its way all the way out to the ocean, carrying our goodbyes and the river's whispers upon its sails.

I realized that what had kept David earthbound for so long wasn't the mystery of his death, but that the person who loved him most hadn't let go.

Art turned in toward me and hugged me; it felt like something a father would do. He pulled back and put his hands on my shoulders and said, "You know, I think

I should call you my 'Second Chance Evie.' … You have given me a second chance, and for that I'm grateful."

Epilogue

It's been a little over a year since Art Carter and I stood by the river and said our goodbyes to David and Nonno. I miss David. Sometimes I find myself looking around town for him, half expecting him to pop up, but he never does. It's at those moments that I realize he's truly gone.

The greatest gift David gave me was his father. My mom and Art married about six months ago. The wedding was small and held in the herb garden at Bliss's house. I couldn't have asked for a more understanding or caring father. He has helped ease some of the pain of missing Nonno and I'd like to think that maybe I help fill some of the space that David left in his heart.

I'm doing my best to live up to the name 'Second Chance Evie.' It's become an ongoing joke between Art and me. Anytime I goof up and do something stupid Art always says, "It's a Good thing that you're Second Chance Evie," and then he gives me another opportunity to do better. I try not to mess it up a second time; I don't want to disappoint him. He's even saved me a few times from my mother's wrath. One time I ducked out of the house to meet Bliss and Johnny to go swim at the river without permission. Art said to my mother, "Ah c'mon Jackie, she won't do it again. She only needs a second chance." He winked at me, and she softened up.

Art's been teaching me how to work with wood and I'm actually pretty good at it. I don't want to make another boat though; anything compared to the last one would seem insignificant. However, we've started making a doll house for Lizzy. I can't wait 'til we give it to her. Sometimes as we carve designs together in the wood, I feel a sense of satisfaction. I think I now understand how Art felt the day he completed Bliss's house.

We're all waiting for the adoption paperwork to get approved. Art and my mom filed for adoption shortly after the wedding, and it means that Art will legally be my father. It's not that I need a piece of paper to tell me that we're a family, but 'Evie Carter' has a nice ring to it.